THE
FIRST
BLACK
TYCOON

TOM MARSHALL

THE FIRST BLACK TYCOON
Copyright 2010 by Thomas S. Marshall,
United States of America

United States Copyright Office Registration Number
TXu 1-729-945
paperback ISBN: 978-1-939166-00-5
epub ISBN: 978-1-939166-02-9
Library of Congress Control Number: 2012948867

PROLOGUE

This fictional novel takes place in the South of the United States just prior to and during the Civil War, a period of approximately ten years from 1858 to 1868.

During this time a slave from Georgia runs away from his plantation due to a dangerous and life threatening situation. Unfortunately because of conditions in the south at that time, including John Brown's attempt at revolution and the advent of the Civil War, he is forced to hide out in plain sight in a neighboring state.

This book details many of the harrowing and sometimes humorous situations he encounters, and his ultimate success in finding freedom and fortune. This novel, while entirely fictional, does include a few historically accurate characters in situations which could have actually taken place.

While I had no personal experience of slavery, both my grandfather and father lived and worked on Barbados plantations. As I grew up, I remembered my father sharing stories of his experiences. His stories included the realities of slavery; the harsh living conditions, the backbreaking labor, the sorrows and heartbreak; but it was the upbeat moments, the laughable anecdotes and memorable characters in and around the sugar cane plantations which he mentioned so often, that I never forgot.

I hope you'll like my story.

ACKNOWLEDGEMENTS

It has been said that everyone has a story inside, waiting to be told. To write that story is daunting. It takes courage, discipline and patience. In the process you second guess yourself, and often become discouraged measuring your work against favored authors, and in the end if you are perseverant, the characters in the novel take on a life of their own, begging for their story to be told and so you press on.

Once completed you are ready to bring your creation into the world. Along the way you realize it was a group effort. I want to acknowledge my group. Thank you, Francine Mullen, friend and typist for accepting the challenge of translating my handwritten copy into a legible form.

Thank you to the best of friends, Dan Kelly and Peter Shamatta for editing and encouragement, and with sincere thanks and appreciation I dedicate this book to Derniere, my wife, for all your assistance, patience and encouragement during this long process. I am truly blessed.

"Opportunity is missed by most people because it comes dressed in overalls and looks like work." — *Thomas Edison*

THE
FIRST
BLACK
TYCOON

THE FIRST BLACK TYCOON

It was 1859, less than two years before the Great War, the battle between the States, or what they would later call the Civil War. The truth is there was nothing civil about that war except that we knew it was coming and that many good men would die.

The reason we knew it was coming was that our owner, Mr. Vanderbilt, told us so. He said, "Because of the financial consideration of the South's economic foundation, war between the States is a foregone inevitability." He always talked like that, using big words that most of the slaves here on this plantation could hardly understand. But the few of us who worked in the Big House, having received a fair education including reading and writing, knew exactly what he meant. We understood the economic conditions of which he spoke, though we pretended not to.

Mr. Vanderbilt was an extremely intelligent Southern gentleman and one of the kindest slave owners in the state of Georgia. He personally taught all of his house servants to read and write and he named us after his heroes from Greek and Roman literature. My name in particular, Tyronious, was some famous Roman senator who warned Caesar that something bad was about to happen. (Unfortunately, Caesar didn't listen and most people know how that story ended.) The other slaves on the plantation just called me Ty. The remainder of this story is about how my name put me in a unique position, saved my life countless times and finally led to my emancipation and fortune.

First let me explain the second half of my name, "Coon". You see our master and owner, no relation to the wealthy industrialist by the same name of Vanderbilt, named all of his darkies and some slaves who were not so very dark, with only one name. For the second name he used the word 'Coon' and in that way he could distinguish us from any White people who might have the same name as us.

During the five or ten years leading up to the war, cotton was king in the South. Most of the slaves on this plantation had jobs planting, cultivating, picking or packing and shipping cotton. Those of us working in the big house had it better than most, since we mainly worked as servants, cleaners, cooks and nannies; and in my particular case as a driver for Mr. Vanderbilt's fine buggy and occasional messenger between the neighboring plantations. Of course I had other duties like assisting my owner with dressing, grooming and physically helping him around the property. All this became more of my work after I left my teen years since by then Mr. Vanderbilt was approaching his seventy-fifth year and wasn't very well.

In the year 1859, two events took place that led me to embark on the adventure of a lifetime and only later did I realize just how lucky I was.

First, Mr. Vanderbilt, my owner, became very sick. He was bedridden, forcing his wife to take over the day to day running of the plantation. This she accomplished by elevating one of the White working men on the farm to the position of overseer. Now believe me this was not a good thing for us slaves who had come to enjoy a reasonably comfortable life, all things considered. At that time, none of us were actually free men and a good position in life wasn't anything for a slave to take for granted.

The new man who became overseer did not particularly like or appreciate the servants working in the Big House for a number of reasons. The truth be told, he was painfully aware that even as slaves and despite our supposedly inferior status we were better educated, better dressed, and more refined than he was. Finally and what probably irked him the most is that my sister and two female cousins and a few other slaves were far better looking than his wife and daughter. And at that time most Southern White men couldn't tolerate such a thing as knowing that we knew and were smart enough to know that he knew we knew.

The second major event during this time was that a foreign investor was reported to be coming to Georgia to invest in a number of small plantations in our area. This financier who was from

Germany, Denmark or Sweden, was shrewdly anticipating the Great War between the States and therefore an eventual disruption in the Southern states exporting cotton to Europe. He figured he could avoid this disruption if he owned shares in a number of plantations. What made this entrepreneur's visit doubly unusual was that this anticipated visitor was a free Black man, educated in England; and commonly referred to as the "*Black Tycoon.*"

Now my friends and family, having seen this story in the local newspapers which Mr. Vanderbilt read and left around the house for the servants, found the similarities hilarious since my name, Tyronius Coon, was usually shortened to "Ty Coon" yet I didn't have two copper coins to rub together.

The main reason I usually didn't have any money, although a good bit ran through my hands, was that I enjoyed what was called at that time, the sporting life. As humble as our small corner of Georgia was, there was always a dance or a party or some horse race or dice game, we called *bones*, and some of the best corn moon-shine available all at reasonable cost. Of course, together they all seemed to separate me from whatever money I may have had.

Approaching my twenty-first birthday in the year of our Lord 1860, I was enjoying my position as driver since my owner was spending more and more time in bed. This left me with his buggy and more free time visiting other plantations picking up medicines and poultices that Mr. Vanderbilt needed and used. Since I was one of a few servants that could travel easily, I had a number of girl-friends on the other plantations in our area, and I was always clean and well-dressed in my owner's old clothes.

I favored his old formal wear since it was always in great shape owing to the fact that he seldom wore them and took great pains to keep them moth free. This was another reason my friends called me Ty Coon, since I usually dressed like a banker. Also, fortunately for me, my owner and I were close to the same size and his old clothes seemed to fit me better than him. In those days, because we had so little of our own, our appearance was very important to us and was very much noticed by our people who lived in similar conditions. All in all, life for me at that time was good but changes were just around the corner.

It all began quite innocently when I decided to visit one of my best looking gal friends on a nearby plantation, under the guise of collecting some Epsom salts from her owner for Mr. Vanderbilt's bad feet.

I figured I could get to the plantation which was eight miles from where I lived, spend some time with Sally and then go up the Big House and inquire about the salts for my owner. What I didn't and couldn't anticipate was that the new overseer's daughter would be there. We called the new overseer of our plantation Mr. Nasty. The daughter was called by the house servants on our plantation, 'Little Miss Nasty' because her manners and appearance were similar to her father.

She apparently had some skills as a pastry chef and was thus employed in this neighboring plantation. But her main objective it seemed in working at this particular farm, was to be close and chase my girlfriend, Sally's, younger brother, Otis; a big brown handsome lad of nineteen.

Although few people would admit it, in those days it wasn't unusual for young White girls to become enamored with young Black boys due to their proximity. But it wasn't safe, especially for the Black boys or any other Black person who was within ear shot of the offending parties. And that, my friends, was exactly the position I found myself in.

I walked into the kitchen anticipating finding Sally preparing dinner. I was hoping to get a little snack as well as possibly a little sugar. But if you consider the possibility of bad timing ruining your life, consider what I walked into: my overseer's daughter wrapped around my girlfriend's brother and trying to stick her tongue into his ear. Not only didn't I want to see this but I didn't want to be in any way associated with it.

Any and every slave knew that this was as much trouble as a non-free person could get into, at that time, without actually killing someone. I knew it could easily lead to a rope tied to a tree and a very dead servant, at the worst. At best, more lashes than any young man would ever need. I knew it was time to go and I hoped that the two people I'd interrupted would be smart enough to keep quiet about having seen me.

Instead, as I turned to leave figuring that it would be better not to wait and see Sally than to place myself in jeopardy by being present where a very serious race crime was taking place, the door at the far end of the kitchen opened and who should enter but Mr. Nasty himself.

His face dropped and I could see a mixture of hatred, revulsion, disbelief and anger. I knew if he had a gun on his person both me and Otis, Sally's brother, might soon be dead. What I didn't know, but soon found out, was that young Miss Nasty had a reputation for chasing roebuck Negroes and her father knew all about it. What I couldn't know is if he realized that I had nothing to do with his daughter and that I was merely a fly on the wall that had entered the room thirty seconds before he did.

Mr. Nasty looked at his daughter and hissed in a low dangerous voice, "You disgust me." He then looked at Otis and said, "Boy, you ought to know better but I guess you couldn't help it. But you'll learn." He finally turned to me and said, "You know you're not in-nocent in all this because I know that you know better with all your education and I'm going to teach you a right proper lesson when I get back to the farm. Now get your sorry ass home, boy and keep your mouth shut about what you saw here today."

I knew right then that my life would never be the same. Either Mr. Nasty was fixing to put some bad stripes on my back that I'd be wearing forever, or in the worst case take me out in the wood some-where and put a bullet in my head, and then bury me somewhere that no one could find me while concocting a story about how I ran away seeking freedom.

While formerly those thoughts were far from my mind, all of a sudden, it all made sense. I had to run and I had to go before Mr. Nasty got back to the plantation tomorrow morning. My plan was simple. Get back to the farm, change horses, say goodbye to my sister, pack some clothes and food, and drive the buggy as far and fast as I could toward the North and freedom. I could just keep going until the slave catchers caught up with me and did whatever that sort of low-life type of people did.

When I returned to the plantation, I told my sister about my predicament and explained that I wasn't leaving forever but long enough for the overseer, Mr. Nasty, to either forget about me or get a job somewhere else. She said she understood but wished I had more options. She gave me most of the money she had which amounted to seventy-five dollars; a small fortune for any person in those days owned by another person. She also made a bunch of biscuits with ham and cheese, three jugs of water and a basket of fried chicken.

I bundled my six suits of clothing with some socks and underwear and my two best pairs of shoes along with a few tools of my trade, a corkscrew, driving gloves, my chauffer's cap and buggy whip.

My sister, having the best handwriting on the plantation, wrote a note instructing me to drive to a plantation where a friend of our owner lived in Delaware. She signed it using Mr. Vanderbilt's signature. I thought this might get me past the slave catchers; but, because I'd never been more than 50 miles from home, I wasn't sure if it would work. I'd heard about slave catchers grabbing free Black men and attempting to sell them back into slavery. I figured that if I ran into them, I might not have a chance even with the best note.

The last thing my sister gave me before we said goodbye is a quill and some ink. She said "Ty, remember to use your head and when you meet strange White men, remember your best manners and posture and look the men straight in the eyes and that way they'll probably believe your lies since you're very good at lying anyway." What I didn't know was just how right she was.

I packed Mr. Vanderbilt's older travelling buggy. It was larger with more storage compartments and rain coverage. I guessed my owner wouldn't miss it as much or as soon since he hadn't been traveling much lately and during the summer months his lighter, newer carriage buggy was the one he preferred. Of course, I knew it was stealing, but since the penalties for a slave running away from home were so severe, I didn't think it could make things much worse and I knew God would forgive me because of the situation I was in.

I hitched up one of my owner's older gray mares which I knew wasn't his favorite figuring that he might not be as mad at me since I didn't run off with his favorite horse. My next thought was to choose a direction.

Remembering what my sister said about using my head, I decided to head west rather than directly east where I thought the slave catchers would expect me to go. The horse I chose was a handsome animal and while not my owners favorite, still quite capable of doing a good job for me in making good my escape from a situation that could only lead to a world of hurt for no one other than yours truly.

I left the plantation close to twelve midnight planning to be at least 20 miles from there by day break. It was by morning turn-out when I knew Mr. Nasty would show up at the farm and I expected to start looking for my sorry behind. While I didn't think much of his intellect, I knew he had a good memory and was a man of his word when it came to punishment for field hands and slaves in general.

Because of the direction I had taken and the distance I was away from my home, I was beginning to enter into unknown territory. After another half hour driving the mare, I decided to stop by a good sized stream and rest a bit, have some breakfast and wash off the dust collected from six straight hours of riding in a horse and buggy.

After feeding and watering my horse and having two biscuits with some water, I removed my clothes and settled down into the stream for what I thought would be a quick bath. No sooner than sitting down in three feet of cool stream water, I heard the voices of two or three young White women who had come along the stream discovering my buggy and were admiring my horse and patting his mane.

Now of course I knew this wasn't my horse and buggy; but for the sake of safety and expediency, I decided to pretend that I was merely on my way home after performing an errand for my owner. Little did I realize that it wouldn't be necessary.

These three young women, after examining my horse and buggy and my packed clothing, finally noticed me in the stream probably 30 feet from where they were standing. One of the bolder girls, I guess she was about 18, called over to me and said, "We were just admiring your coach and stead. We seldom see buggies like this around here anymore. What is your name young man and where are you from?"

Without even thinking I replied in my best educated English, "I'm Ty Coon and I'm from ..."

"You don't need to tell us anymore", she giddily interrupted. "We've read about you in the papers for the last two months and are happy to see you've found your way to our part of Georgia. Is there anything that you need?"

She then asked, "Would you like to come up to our father's plantation; it's just a quarter mile down the road?" While the offer of hospitality was no doubt sincere, I had every desire to put as many miles between myself and Mr. Nasty as soon as I possibly could.

I slowly walked out of the stream apologizing to the young ladies for being unable to stay and visit right now due to a previous appointment but that I would be returning within a week and would be glad to stop by then to make the acquaintance of their father.

I noticed the girl who had originally spoken to me, a buxom lass, had a fixed eye on my personal equipment as I walked out of the stream toward my buggy. Her eyes grew wider and she said to me, "Mr. Tycoon you have the largest fandangle I have ever seen." I really didn't know what to say since I really didn't know how many fandangles this young White woman had in fact seen.

Not wanting to seem unsophisticated, while remembering what my sister said about being smart, I replied that my mother had always said that what she called a fandangle was my greatest wealth. This caused the young White woman to smile and ask if I enjoyed sharing my wealth. I knew exactly what she meant, but pretended I did not and instead replied, "I certainly like to invest my wealth and make it grow."

She quickly replied, "I think I could probably help you with that when you stop by in the next week."

That was as good as any undisguised offer I had in quite a while. In spite of it all, I realized that any delay might put me into the hands of my revengeful overseer and I could hardly afford that. So I thanked her for the offer and told her I would make every effort to see her and her father in one week's time.

Feeling refreshed and excited and not the least bit bothered by leading the girls on, I headed my buggy in the opposite direction of where the girls had pointed to their farm and soon found myself riding through some of the prettiest countryside I had ever encountered. Rows of corn, tobacco and cotton, stretched on for miles with an occasional field of melons thrown in, I'm sure, by the field hands who enjoyed them so much.

Our people being a great deal smarter than our owners suspected, often planted additional crops in out-of-the-way places so we could enjoy a cool melon on a hot day working the fields, far from home. It was in one of these small melon patches that my next adventure took place. After riding in the buggy for about three hours, I decided to rest next to a small patch of melons planted close to a larger field of sugar cane.

I fed and watered my horse and had just collected what I thought was the best melon in the field when up rode three of the most dangerous looking White men I'm sure any runaway slave had ever seen. Not only were they big, dirty, and ugly, but they smelled to high heaven and had probably only six or eight teeth between the three of them.

These White men had pistols, rifles, ropes, whips, manacles and leg irons. The few teeth they had were all badly stained with chewing tobacco and may not have been brushed or cleaned since before I was born. To say they were scary was a far understatement. Their horses even looked mean, if such a thing is possible.

They rode right up to me and surrounded me. While I was scared to death, an idea immediately came to me from out of the blue. I looked at the roughest of the hoodlums while pretending that I didn't recognize them as slave catchers and said in my best English grammar, "Sir, if you're the owner of this beautiful little garden patch, I'd be glad to pay you for your fine melon. In fact," said I, "I'd be willing to buy some produce from you on a steady basis given the opportunity."

The three men looked baffled. Then the leader of the group said, "No. We don't own shit. We just work for people who do. What's yer name boy?"

I looked him in his eye straightened my shoulders, and said, "Sir, I am Ty Coon and I am pleased to make your acquaintance."

At that moment, the scoundrel on his left spoke up with, "Well damn boy we heard a you. You be the Black Tycoon that evabody is talkin about. What you doing round these parts anyhow?"

I said, "Sir, I'm looking for investment opportunities in order to prevent the disruption of the flow of materials necessary for my business activities."

While the bafflement remained in their expressions, their demeanor relaxed and I sensed a totally different attitude toward me by their posture and bearing.

They began calling me '*Mr. Tycoon*' and explained that they were employed by a plantation owner some 80 miles south of where we were and were attempting to retrieve some property that had been misplaced. I imagined they were couching their language in a somewhat unsophisticated attempt at not insulting my European sensibilities. Still I didn't trust the leader of this group of ragamuffins and decided to play what I considered my hole card.

I motioned to the three men before taking my melon knife out of a box on the buggy and asked if they'd like to enjoy some of this beautiful melon with me. I then mentioned that I'd hope they wouldn't mind me removing my shirt since I didn't know how long it would be before I could find a decent laundress to clean my clothes, this far out in the country.

My hole card was that because I'd always lived with the same kindly owner, I had nary a stripe from whippings on my person. In those days, runaway slaves were often identified by the number of stripes that they wore on their backs. The men watching me certainly noticed as I turned to hang my shirt inside the buggy carriage. Everyone knew that names could be easily changed, but stripes from a whip would stay with you to the grave.

The three body snatchers declined my offer of the melon and bid me good luck with my investing. I wasn't sure if they didn't want to eat with me because of my color or the fact that they would rather drink their lunch from a liquor bottle. In those days, bad manners and bad intentions were easily confused.

After finishing a good portion of that delicious melon, I headed off in a different direction from that of the odiferous saddle tramps. I wasn't sure any longer of the direction I was taking since this was the second time I'd changed direction in an unfamiliar area. I was confident, however, that I would be able to realign myself when the stars came out that evening and I was sure that I was heading for an even greater adventure next.

I was lucky travelling on the back roads for the rest of the day, uneventfully not passing a single person. That night when the stars came out, I realized that I was only a little

off my desired course and I could easily get back on track with a slight adjustment tomorrow.

The next morning after breakfast and a bath, I headed across a meadow that I thought would correct my direction. After a few miles, or as many as eight, I came upon what I thought was an abandoned horse and wagon with one wheel broken and splintered. When I slowed beside it, a young woman barely older than me came out of the woods and called to me. She said, "Can you help me young man? I seem to have had a mishap and I am really at a loss, though I'm not far from my home."

She told me she was sure she had another wheel at home for the wagon but there wasn't anyone home to help her. Her husband had gone off to Atlanta to settle some family business and the hired help only worked when her husband was there to pay them. She then inquired as to my name and address and could I be of assistance.

I told her my name was Ty Coon and my address, as of this moment, was on the road between plantations. She said that she thought she had heard my name mentioned before but couldn't remember by who or what they might have said. I replied that I'd be glad to help but unfortunately, I also didn't have a spare wheel with me. I mentioned I could give her a ride to her place, get the wheel and return her here and assist her if it was absolutely necessary, since she mentioned she lived nearby.

Most White people at the time felt if a reputable White person asked a slave or servant for assistance, it was traditionally required that the slave help them, if at all possible. Whatever time was lost from the slave's normal job or labor was to be reimbursed by the person he helped and they would pay such monies according to the time someone else's servant agreed to help them, even if the person who needed the help insisted on it.

When I helped her into my carriage I noticed that she, in addition to being well dressed and quite attractive, was also a fairly tall woman built along the lines of the field workers in that she was solid and better muscled and in much better shape than the average White woman. In fact she looked like an athlete or some sort of dancer.

Her house was less than a mile away but it took us some time since it was located in fairly deep woods at the end of a large number of small winding roads that seemed to go nowhere except deeper into the woods.

In pulling up to the front of her farm house, I noticed that the building, while handsome, seemed to have had little maintenance and repair for a number of years. The grounds also were sorely lacking and would best be described as *gone to seed*.

Mrs. Appleby, or Alice as I later learned, while climbing down and off my buggy, caught her heel in a side step and fell into my arms as I was assisting her out of the carriage.

Fortunately, I was in the right position when she fell and I caught her despite her probably weighing as much as I, although I would never mention a lady's weight. For a moment we were clutching each other fairly close. As soon as Alice caught her breath, she smiled and said, "Well you certainly are a strong lad Mr. Tycoon."

I was a little bit surprised that she remembered my name, but my sister always warned me that a lot of women only play dumb to see how far they can get. I slowly started to look around more cautiously and I immediately noticed a bunch of newspapers on top of a side cupboard in the front parlor. I guessed if Mrs. Appleby had actually heard my name before, it was probably from the newspaper while reading about my namesake and not me.

She remarked that I must be very handy around a house since I drove such a lovely carriage and she knew how strong I was. I mixed this information in my brain with the condition of the grounds and need for maintenance on the exterior of the house and I began wondering exactly what this woman was sizing me up for. Mrs. Appleby brought me a glass of lemonade and told me she would be out in a minute. She just wanted to change so she could help me find the spare wheel in the barn.

While waiting for Mrs. Appleby, I looked at the photographs on the mantle to see if there were any of her and her husband and children. The only picture there was of her and a man who looked old enough to be her father.

I hadn't heard her walk up behind me because she had taken her shoes off. In fact, she had taken almost all of her clothing off except what we used to call, in those days, unmentionables. She smiled at me and put her hands on my shoulders and said, "I see you noticed those pictures of me and my husband and yes he is quite a bit older than me." She then explained, "I met him when I was a young dancer and the idea of living in a big house on my own farm appealed to me. I didn't really know how boring it could be."

"But you, Mr. Tycoon, I think you and I could do some fine things together that might turn out to be both profitable and fun."

'Whoa Nelly' went through my head, but I have to admit the situation was both exciting and dangerous. Could I get into any more trouble? *Should* I get into any more trouble? Would I like to get into any more trouble; and what type of trouble exactly could I get into anyway?

Mrs. Appleby was on me like white on rice or in my case white on coal. I was committing any number of race crimes from just being alone with a White woman in her unmentionables, from reckless eyeballing, to speaking to a White lady concerning lewd and immoral perversions related to illegal sexual co-mingling of the races.

They would hang me and my horse and I doubt that all my body parts would still be attached if I was lucky enough to have a decent burial. Still, I was also wondering what she meant when she said we could have some fun and it could also be profitable. I said to her,

"Mrs. Appleby, may I call you Alice?" "Of course", she said, "and I'll call you Ty."

"Good. My question to you, Alice, is what exactly did you have in mind when you said we might do something profitable?" At the same time as we were having this conversation I was staring at one of the greatest bodies I had ever seen on a female of any color or nationality. She had it all. Built like a brick outhouse, everything that Uncle John needs, with all the bells and whistles in all the right places. She was young and lean, firm, tall, and beautiful. She had a peaches and cream complexion with long straight black hair that was down to her shoulder blades. I sighed.

If reckless eyeballing was a serious crime, and it was, what I was doing was a capital offense punishable by hanging, a firing squad, and then some rednecks on horses trampling my sorry ass. I had very mixed emotions about staying or leaving. My head said to go while my *little head* said 'wait a minute, let's stay a while longer.'

Mrs. Appleby or Alice saw that I was in a dilemma and started to explain exactly what she had in mind. She said that while her farm had once been quite a profitable spread, her husband's advancing age and frequent bouts of illness caused by rheumatism and gout had left them close to destitution. She went on to explain that not only couldn't her husband do much work around the farm, but he couldn't do any work in their bedroom at all.

While this information was more than I wanted to know, I wondered still how she felt I could fit into this dilemma. Alice explained that after meeting me, she remembered reading about me in one of the newspapers Mr. Appleby had brought home from his frequent trips to the doctor in Atlanta where he was at this very minute. She went on to say that she had been acting coy when she said she thought she had heard my name but couldn't remember where. Her proposal was that I invest in her farm and I would be rewarded with not only a quarter of the best bottom country cotton fields but some of the best acrobatic bedroom privileges any young boy of my race could ever imagine.

All the while I had been leering at her long beautiful legs and dancer's body and realized that her last statement was probably the truest thing she had said so far. To be perfectly honest, I was lost at that moment. I decided to do something that I should have realized was dangerous and illegal in more than a dozen different ways.

By then Alice had both her arms around me and one leg coiled around my lower body. She was so close that there wasn't room for the Holy Ghost between us. She was so warm that a country boy like me felt it would be better to take his clothes off so he didn't get all sweaty.

She must have read my mind because the next thing she said was "Let me help you get out of your things." She had my buttons undone and my shirt and trousers off so fast I thought she must also be a magician. Again, she read my mind and said, "Don't worry. I've had a small amount of experience at this type of thing when I was a dancer before I met my husband."

She then quipped, "You like riding don't you? Well, I'm going to take you on the ride of your life. In fact, it's what we used to call in New Orleans, where I worked, 'around the world.'"

I'm not exaggerating when I tell you that for the next three or four hours, I was introduced to many customs from places in the world like France, Greece and even China that

I had never seen or heard of before but I was more than willing to revisit again and again.

Alice told me that she thought I had an exceptional love sausage and while I'd never heard anyone calling that part of my anatomy by that name before, I had also never met anyone who seemed to like to try to almost swallow it either. Her acrobatic performance had me stretched out in more ways than are imaginable. My personal equipment seemed to stay harder than Chinese arithmetic. At the end of what seemed like the better part of the day, Mrs. Alice Appleby said to me, "Ty, I think you and I should be business partners since I can see now that you could provide me with some unanticipated benefits that I hadn't expected but I surely appreciate."

As my heart rate began to return to normal, I suddenly remembered my sister's admonition to use my head and intelligence. I nonchalantly asked Alice what amount of money it would take for me to invest in her farm. I knew the price would be inflated but since, at that time, slaves couldn't own anything, I figured nothing ventured anything gained. At least I would gain some valuable information about property. As soon as we began talking business, Alice surprised me and spoke intelligently about cost projections, the coming war's effect and how they would relate to me.

Mrs. Appleby told me that the cost of prime farm land was now approximately four acres per dollar. She anticipated that if the war that everyone knew was inevitable lasted as long as two years, the price would come down drastically because of the flow of commerce being disrupted. However following the war, prices would shoot up drastically due to the increase in demand for cotton and good farm land. Figuring all these different intangibles in, she said that if we combined some of our shipping cost following the down time, she could probably sell me some prime acreage at 4 1/2 acres per dollar.

I quickly did some computations in my head and decided that if I parted with $50 of the $75 I had in my possession, I could own, along with my sister, nearly 225 acres of land with a stream going right through it. Of course, this depended on slaves being granted freedom during the conflict and this is something that my owner, Mr. Vanderbilt, had already predicted while warning us house servants to keep it under our hats so that the rednecks didn't get angry and try to kill us before our lucky day.

With this in mind, and realizing that much of this was speculation, I decided to gamble on good fortune and asked Mrs. Appleby if she could sign a bill of sale without her husband being there. She explained that the plantation was already in her name because her husband was so much older than her and worried about dying before her. She also agreed to show me the deed to the property to put my mind at ease.

We took care of our business and then took care of some more business, if you get my meaning. Finally around dusk we went out to retrieve Mrs. Appleby's horse and wagon. During the time I was replacing the wheel on Alice's wagon, some riders from one of the nearby plantations rode up on us and for a moment I questioned the wisdom and folly of having spent the day with Mrs. Appleby.

But when they approached and saw me in what was obviously a subservient position of changing a wagon wheel while Alice was sitting comfortably on my fine carriage observing my labor, they simply said, "It seems that you have everything in hand, Mrs. Appleby." To which Alice replied, "Thank you for your concern. I assure you I'm in good hands." The riders went on their way.

I spent the next week on Alice's farm doing quite a few small repairs around the place that were needed. I also enjoyed many of the benefits of our new partnership and found that Mrs. Appleby was not only talented in the bedroom but also a skilled baker of cakes and pies and other delicious confections. I would even go as far as to say that her pies were as good as any I had ever tasted.

Unfortunately, or not, I had miles to go before I could feel comfortable about not being grabbed by the hooligan slave catchers. Alice's husband was due home soon and I'm sure that there was already a reward posted for my return in the local Georgia newspapers. I packed my clothes, borrowed a spare wheel from my new business partner, looked around my new, although recent and temporary home, wishing to see it again, and bid Alice goodbye. Before I left, Alice made me a large basket of food to take and added three large pies.

I left her with the address of one of my cousins in the Carolinas who I knew would always be stationary since he lived on a farm on an island. She also gave me an address in Savannah, Georgia where one of her girlfriends had a clothing shop, through which I could get in touch with her if I wanted to contact her without her husband knowing.

My plan, although not formalized at this point, was to head for either New Orleans or Baltimore. At the time, both places had the largest free Black population. I had heard of both Harriet Tubman and her underground railroad to freedom and Frederick Douglas, the great Black orator and race champion; and I hoped that somehow through sheer luck come hell or high water, I would be able to connect with one of these active heroes and thus gain assistance in my pursuit of liberty.

Only then did I realize that what I was now pursuing was not only reprieve from punishment and oppression, but actually freedom itself. Many of us, while constantly dreaming of escape, were reluctant to leave our family and friends, with little or no funds and even less connections in a free world which we had only heard of but had never actually seen.

My next few days had me traveling the back roads adjacent to Hen Cart Road, which in turn led to Savannah on the eastern side. On the other side of Georgia, the western side was Tuscaloosa, Mobile, or New Orleans. The time passed uneventfully and I passed few travelers who for the most part preferred the new, larger, more traveled road that I was avoiding as much as possible. My days were spent riding and resting the horse occasionally near a stream or river, while my nights were spent mainly hiding with my buggy pulled far enough into the woods that only the birds and wild animals could notice I was there. I avoided the better cultivated fields and detoured around any small villages that I could see I was approaching from road signs and advertisements for lodging and victuals.

Even though it was somewhat out of my way, I decided to stop in Savannah and see if I could locate any news of the assistance I needed or if there was already a reward offered for the recapture of Tyronius Coon. I'd been gone now for close to a week and wasn't really sure of how fast news traveled in the outside world. I didn't know anyone in Savannah, but since Mrs. Appleby had given me the name and address of Victoria, her friend and seamstress, I decided to try and find her.

The city of Savannah was an eye opener for me since I was a poor, but well educated, country bumpkin. I never realized what an intense place these cities could really be.

I had never seen so many people crowded together other than at large horse races. And even then, everyone was outside in the fresh air. It seemed to me that this city had no rhyme or reason. The buildings were built right alongside of each other with many even sharing only a wall between them.

Some of the buildings were four stories high and I couldn't imagine why anyone would want to climb so many stairs every day of their life. I wondered if these people had special servants whose only job was to carry things up and down the stairs for them. At the same time, I had never seen so many Black people in one place moving about so freely, like they all had some place to go but somewhere different than everyone else.

I noticed a number of other Black carriage drivers who tipped their caps to me in passing, but didn't speak. I knew the street I was looking for, but soon realized that with the vastness of this city I could be here for days without locating it. Since I didn't have a map I decided to pull up behind another driver who had stopped and ask directions.

As soon as I approached him and asked my question, he said, "Country cousin, you must be new in town!" He continued, "The place you're looking for is in the Red Light District on the waterfront. I'd be careful down there at night and even more careful if you get close to any of those working gals. They're a slippery fingered lot, if you know what I mean." He then gave me some simple directions and I thanked him and went on my way. I hoped to be there and gone before dark since he told me to be careful in a serious tone. Advice like that I didn't want to ignore.

I pulled up in front of Victoria's building in my buggy and no-ticed a small sign that said '*Clothing and Accessories, Custom Fitted.*' I tied my horse to the post out front and entered a small neatly kept shop with a bell attached to the door that rang when you entered. A young and beautiful mixed race girl came out from behind a curtain and asked, "Can I help you sir?"

I mentioned that I had recently met a woman, Mrs. Alice Appleby, who recommended her as a fine seamstress whom I should look up if I was ever in the vicinity of Savannah. She smiled, introduced herself as "Victoria" and said she was glad to hear from someone who had seen her friend, since she had not seen or heard a word from her since Alice got married some two and a half years ago. Victoria inquired about Alice's health and wellbeing and then asked what I had in mind by way of her services, being that she only made woman's clothing and accessories.

Not wanting to jump right into my need for meeting people who could help me escape, I mentioned that I might be interested in some woman's clothing for my sister. Victoria again smiled and said, "I'm not sure your sister would want the type of clothes I design."

I wondered what type of clothes Victoria designed and asked her what she made or was it a woman's secret. Just then a police wagon with Savannah Police Department stenciled on the side pulled up behind my carriage and two large White policemen began climbing down. Victoria saw them through the window, looked at me quizzi-cally and whispered, "Quick, come behind the counter if you're not alright with the law."

She didn't have to tell me twice. As I slid behind the counter, she quickly motioned for me to crawl under her hoop skirt and be very quiet.

The two policemen came in and inquired if she had seen the carriage driver that had parked his horse and buggy in front of her shop. Victoria answered she had noticed him leave the carriage and go down the street, but she didn't know where. She further inquired if she should be alarmed or in any jeopardy because of him. The policemen said no but they noticed that he wasn't displaying a Hackney license and unless he was only a personal driver for a private party, he needed one to operate in the city of Savannah.

During this time while hiding under Victoria's hoop skirt, I of course noticed her shapely legs and while momentarily trying not to look, I couldn't resist and peeked at her beautiful bottom and discovered exactly what Victoria's secret was. It was the most beautiful set of undergarment unmentionables that any man had ever seen. Or in my case the most heavenly made undergarments that I had ever been close enough to touch.

They were flimsy and bright with lace and little ribbons and material so light that it resembled confection that could melt in your mouth. I truly believed that they were intentionally made to make a man's mouth water, but not necessarily for food.

The policemen left but said they'd be back in an hour to see if the carriage was still there. Less than a minute after I heard the policemen leave, Victoria spoke down to me, "You can come out now and I hope you won't mention the unusual position you were in with me."

"Of course not," I replied, "but now I think I know your secret. Those unmentionables you're wearing are the most beautiful ladies garments I've ever seen."

Victoria blushed, "You have in fact discovered my secret, but it's fairly well known by half the dancers, courtesans, kept women, and higher class working girls from here to New Orleans."

"That's how I met Alice before she was Mrs. Appleby and that's how I knew you could be trusted. What is it that you're really after since I know you're not here to buy some of my custom made fanny huggers?" Victoria asked.

"Well", I confessed, "I'm in a bit of a predicament and I could use any help or information I could get in order to distance myself from Georgia and, if at all possible, get up North to the Free states."

"Say no more," she said, I can't possibly help you since many of us have that same dream and I haven't been able to help myself either."

"What I can do for you though" she continued," is give you some good information that may keep you out of trouble and harm's way for a long enough time for you to figure it out in terms of exactly where you want to go and how, with some luck, you can get there."

She explained that most people running away from the south were caught at night traveling on back roads when everyone and anyone, especially the runaway slave catchers, knew they shouldn't be. The lesson was, whenever possible travel in the day light. She explained that most people escaped by water routes and without money; and, even more importantly, connections with good directions. It was close to impossible in spite of the small number of folks who had been successful.

Victoria mentioned Harriet Tubman, the legendary head of the Underground Railroad, and said that she often came through Savannah although few knew in advance, and because of her great skills of deception could be standing next to you in a saloon without your being able to recognize her. She mentioned that Mrs. Tubman sometimes frequented an ale house two blocks over from where we were but often dressed as an older man and, in most cases, couldn't be found unless she intended to be.

She also warned me about Black con men that would promise you the world and then sell you into the hands of the slave catchers, who would give them a small portion of the reward. The give-a-way for these con men, she said, was that they usually asked if you had any money and tried to get you to pay them a finder's fee for putting you in touch with someone who knew someone who could put you onto the Underground Railroad.

She also told me a story she had heard about a slave named Henry (Box) Brown who it was said was nailed into a cargo box and shipped to freedom on a boat. What allowed him to be successful is that Mrs. Tubman knew some Black seamen who handled and unloaded the cargo on this boat.

When Victoria looked at the grandfather clock on the wall, she mentioned that the two policemen said they would soon be back

THE FIRST BLACK TYCOON

and that I'd better be on my way. I thanked her for her help and told her I might again be in touch and that if I saw Alice any time soon, I would send her regards along. Victoria smiled and, placing a long finger against her lips, the last thing she said before I left was, "Don't forget to keep my secret."

Leaving her shop I noticed the police wagon turn a corner three blocks down and head in my direction. Rather than getting in my buggy and risk being stopped and questioned, I decided to slip through a nearby alley and stop by the Ale House Victoria had mentioned Mrs. Tubman frequented. Good fortune was obviously smiling on me that day because while I didn't really know what direction the ale house was in, I soon found it almost by accident. In passing what appeared to be a shabby warehouse I noticed a sign on a door that said,

SEAMENS ALE HOUSE
We serve Colored and Chinese but if you don't have coin
Get Gone.

The sign also warned that no habitual drunkards, brawlers, pickpockets, sneaky drink thieves, moochers or shit bums need enter. I'd heard of most of these types of people except sneaky drink thieves, which I assumed was someone that would drink from your glass if you went out to use the comfort station.

It took me a minute for my eyes to adjust to the darkness in the ale house; but as they did, I realized that there was a good crowd of people here for such an early hour in the day. When I said a good crowd, I didn't mean in any way good looking. This crowd was rough, made up mainly of one quarter drunk seamen from all over the world, and the rest a nefarious group that could have been involved in any sort of crimes including but not limited to murder. Even the women, and there were quite a few, looked rough; although some were attractive in a rough sort of way.

I knew from reading that in the best bars in New Orleans a glass of beer might cost you a nickel, but in this type of low life establishment you could probably get a shot of whiskey and a beer chaser, what some called a boiler maker, for one or two pennies. It seemed, however, no amount of money could get you a clean glass. Noticing that, I decided to order a bottle of beer.

As soon as my beer arrived, three or four young ladies brushed by me and asked if I'd like some company. I wasn't used to this much attention from strange women, but I thought that if I said yes they would probably expect me to offer to buy them a drink and I didn't want any part of what that might lead to. What I was looking for was information. After only five minutes in there, I decided it was probably the wrong time and/or a hopeless cause due to bad timing.

Just seconds after I had decided to leave but before I could get up to go, a rather well dressed young man around my own age addressed me as country cousin and asked if I had a minute or two for some informative conversation. I said certainly and he sat down across from me. He said he noticed that I declined the company offered me by the several girls that had approached me and wondered if I had something else in mind. He went on that he could see from my bearing and dress that I was obviously a well-educated and cultured gentleman of color and obviously employed by wealthy cultured White folk. He didn't understand however, why I didn't realize that romance without finance was nonsense. That is, of course, unless I wandered into this fine sporting establishment for something other than romance.

This fast talking young man by the name of Donald went on to say, "Money makes the world go around and if you aren't there you must be square."

I had no idea what he was talking about, but I realized that city people had a language of their own. And my Black brothers always seemed to come up with innovative ideas for turning proper English into something else. Donald continued on saying, "A man could do badly all by himself, and it is commonly known that it is better to be alone than in bad company. That is", and here he smiled lecherously, "unless you were looking for some bad company."

He then offered, "If I can be so bold, since we've only met a few minutes ago, what exactly are you looking for cousin?"

This fellow, Donald, was the second best dressed man in the ale house after me; and since he certainly didn't appear as larcenous as the people around him, I decided to trust him a little and cautiously told him what I was looking for in a round-about fashion.

I said, "Donald, I'm looking for information that might help me relocate out of the state of Georgia. Is that something that you might be able to help me with?"

His eyes lit up and while I wasn't sure he understood what I was asking, he assured me that there wasn't anything he couldn't help me with given that I had financial resources available.

He said that he was an entrepreneur, inventor, songwriter, and man about town and that he could do or get anything anyone needed, including a ticket and safe passage to anywhere as far as Timbuktu. I wasn't sure if that was a song he just made up or if he could actually get me, through his connections, safe passage to somewhere far away.

Donald looked at me satisfied and said, "No problem cousin, I can have you heading wherever you want to go by the week's end. I'll only need a small down payment for some friends of mine that work on the ships sailing out of Savannah." He said he was going to use the comfort station out back, but when he returned we could discuss where I wanted to go and exactly how much I could afford to put down for my passage.

Bingo, thank heavens Victoria had warned me. As I finished my beer and started to get up from the table, an older gentleman put his hand on my shoulder and said, "Young man, you better come with me before that conman, Donald, gets back. He's fixing to put the slave catchers on your trail and it's just a matter of time before you'll be wearing leg irons and new stripes on your back!"

This old colored man wore a butler's suit and the smoothest complexion of any person that age that I'd ever seen. While his hands looked strong, he was thin as a bone and, except for his shoulders, wasn't much bigger than a small woman. His voice and demeanor however, had the tone of authority and leadership that could not be disguised. I knew right then that this was the *Black Moses*, Harriet Tubman.

We quickly left through the front door and after taking a few turns, arrived in front of Victoria's shop where we got into my carriage buggy and drove off immediately. I asked how she knew this was my buggy and that I had left it here. She just smiled and said Victoria had more secrets than a lot of people knew.

Harriet went on to explain that after watching me come into the ale house, a message had been sent to her warning her to look out for me and what my situation was. She further explained that because of John Brown's recent raid on the federal arsenal at Harper's Ferry, this was the worst time in recent history for anyone in my situation to try to escape. At the same time, she said she could understand the position I was in and even though she was shutting down her own operations for a couple of months, she could possibly help me with information and contacts if I could somehow manage to get myself to certain places along the border of Free states.

We discussed several different possible routes to freedom, but time and again came back to the fact that at the moment, the White southerners were scared senseless and this was the worst possible time for a Black man traveling alone in the South.

Harriet, after looking over the forged traveling documents written by my sister, said they would fool probably half of the people that stopped me. She explained the other half, however, couldn't read; and in many instances, would just as soon rob a well off servant, sell his horse and buggy and bury him off the road in the woods where no one would be the wiser. Especially in the case of someone being a great distance from their owner's home.

After debating my dilemma for a long while, Harriet said that she thought my best bet was to take the coastal route to New Orleans and try to hide out there for a while in the free Black community.

She and everyone else in politics was anticipating the war between the states and knew that it would open up many unforeseen opportunities that until then no one could imagine.

She also mentioned that a number of our people, who were former slaves, had escaped to Florida and moved in with the Seminole Indians. Since I was heading in that direction anyway, it might be something to consider.

I was so busy concentrating on what Harriet was telling me that I hardly noticed when I came up on the very same two policemen that had been looking for me earlier at Victoria's shop. They recognized my buggy and told me to pull over. They said they were looking for me earlier to inquire if I picked up passengers without having a hackney license or was I employed by a private individual?

Their appearance had surprised me so much that I was momentarily flustered and speechless. Though I was normally quite good at telling tales, at that moment I couldn't get the tongue in my mouth to move in any direction.

I really didn't have to worry, however, for right then I saw an example of how the Black Moses could seemingly work miracles. Mrs. Tubman, in her disguise as a man, spoke up to the policeman closest to us in the wagon said, "Young man, you're out of the Fourth District on Canal Street are you not?"

"Yes, I am," was his reply.

"Well, I know your sergeant in there, Mr. Finery, and if you ask him he'll tell you this young man works for me exclusively. I'm Dr. Brown from Mortimer Lane in the Sixth District. The only people beside myself that ride in my carriage are those patients of mine with cholera or other infectious diseases, and none of them pay so I see no need for my driver to acquire a hackney license. If there are any illnesses or infirmaries in your family, drop by my place. I don't mind working on White folks and its half price for policemen and other civil employees."

The policemen, having heard clients with *cholera* riding in this buggy, were glad to see the last of us. They thanked us for our time and expressed, "Good luck!"

Harriet explained that they'd never mention it to their sergeant since he was notoriously foul tempered and only spoke to the patrolmen when he was issuing orders or chewing them out. She also told me that if I was going to spend time anywhere it was always a good idea to remember the names of important people so you could keep your lies straight, and the bolder your lies the better.

I left Harriet off on a street not far from where we were. The houses were stately and expensive and I was sure only White people lived in this part of Savannah. I'm also sure they had slaves and servants and Harriet Tubman could fit in anywhere from Boston's Back Bay to the waterfront docks of Savannah, Georgia.

What was then called the Southern Route to freedom was the route Harriet had suggested and what we both felt given the considerations of the time was best suited for me and my health and survival. I was considering if it was possible for me to get as far away as New Orleans, if it was possible to integrate myself instead into the Indian nations in Florida or if I had any other options.

For close to a month now, I had been away from what had been my home for my entire life. I missed my family and friends dearly. I also missed my bed as humble as it was and

was growing tired of meals made up of pilfered vegetables and melons.

I drove my buggy aimlessly for a number of miles and stopped beside a beautiful little lake that I happened upon, where I decided to spend the night. After feeding and watering my horse and trying to conceal my carriage as best I could, I settled down to a somewhat restless slumber that I'd hoped would lead me to dream about what I should do next.

When I awoke at dawn, I heard some young people talking not far from where I was and quickly realized that they were on a small row boat that was drifting on the lake not far from where I had concealed myself and my buggy.

They appeared to be fishing and looked much like myself and the other field hands their age that lived on my plantation. I called out to them and asked if they'd caught anything that they might be willing to sell.

They quickly paddled over to the shore close to where I was and produced a fine large catfish that they said they would be glad to sell or barter if I had anything worth trading. I wasn't sure what I had that would interest them. Then I remembered the pies Alice had packed for me and realized that I had one left. Having already eaten the other two and having enjoyed them immensely, I figured this last one might work to enable a change in my diet.

I suggested a pie for a fish and the two young men agreed instantly. In fact, they were glad to clean and cook the fish for me as part of the bargain. People in bondage in those days were eager to talk to strangers of their own race since news from different people who had been different places and seen and heard different things was at times, and in many cases, all the news we received.

As the fish cooked, they asked how far I had traveled and what news I had heard about politics, the coming election for president, and if I felt that the possibility of Senator Lincoln becoming President of the United States would actually lead to a separation and war between the North and the South?

I realized that these young field hands were a great deal more intelligent than their owners probably would give them credit for. At the same time, I knew that many of our people would often feign ignorance as a protective measure to keep White folk comfortable and less suspicious of them.

My information about Senator Lincoln was limited to what I had read in the local Southern papers referring to him as a "Black Republican and an enemy of the Southern way of life. I had no idea if he was popular in the North, although I suspected as much.

I mentioned that I had heard something about the Fugitive Slave Act of 1850 being increasingly resisted in the North and that many Southerners feared that if Mr. Lincoln was elected that the law would be abolished and the kidnapping of former slaves (which were still considered stolen property in the South) would become much more difficult or nearly impossible.

One of the two boys I was talking to said that what we needed was a Black president. I asked him how he thought that could happen since most of us weren't free and couldn't vote anyway. He said in his mind it was simple, all you have to do is get enough White men to run for the same office at one time, then the voters get confused and when their favorite candidate gets knocked out of the running, they all vote for the last candidate that they thought could win. This, of course, would be the one Black candidate in the election.

I said he had a good point but I was afraid that it would be a long time into the future if we ever saw that day at all. In fact, I thought, we'll probably see plain water being sold in bottles before then, and carriages with steam engines like locomotives.

Our conversations went many different ways and included what I had recently seen in the city of Savannah. Finally, I casually brought our conversation around to the question of travel to New Orleans by small boat and if they thought it possible.

These two young men, I later learned, both three to five years younger than me, were brothers whose last name was Jangles, a common Dutch name that their owner had and they shared. They also had never been far from their home plantation and although they had heard of the fine mixed race girls that worked in the New Orleans sporting houses and dance halls and dreamed of visiting such a place, hadn't any idea of how far away it was or how long it would take to get there.

The younger of the two brothers, Beauregard Jangles, the

comedian, said he'd love to go there and work as an entertainer dancing and singing. He was sure that given the coming war and manumission following, he could make a very good living entertaining White people there. He also felt he could definitely have a good time entertaining the café au lait working girls in that area during his off time since he'd already worked out a routine and had picked out his stage name 'Bo Jangles'. I humorously said that I thought it was a great idea and I was sure that I'd be reading about him in the entertainment section of the newspapers in the not too distant future. My immediate concern, however, was how to get to New Orleans from where we were.

The brothers speculated that I'd need a good sized boat just to carry the provisions needed for what they guessed would be, at the very least, a two-week voyage. That was, of course, if I were going to make the trip without coming back to shore while sailing around the coast. Also they added I'd have to have a fairly good knowledge of sailing since the wind certainly wouldn't always be blowing in the direction I wanted to go. Finally, they said not only would I need a great deal of money to hire such a boat, but even if I could, I certainly couldn't trust any Black sailors to deliver me safely anywhere. They were mainly all a half step away from being pirates and once at sea wouldn't hesitate to separate me from any possessions I might have and put me overboard.

The young comedian, Beau, said, "I'm sure you've heard that dead men tell no tales." I had heard just such a thing and also that Black sailors were some of the most notorious scoundrels to be found anywhere because the nature of their work kept them in the company of other desperados who wouldn't hesitate to separate a fool from his money; and I didn't want to be that fool.

Remembering the group of roughnecks I had encountered in the Seaman's Ale House in Savannah, and knowing better than to condemn all men in one profession for the sins of a few, I began to worry more and more about my decision to travel to New Orleans and how I would reach my destination. So far I had been both lucky and comfortable traveling in my owner's horse and buggy. But I knew that it was just a matter of time until the advertisements concerning runaway slaves would include a description of the buggy and the gray mare that I had absconded with. This, of course, would make it very dangerous for me and I feared for any other servant, as well, who might be legitimately driving his owner's carriage pulled by a gray mare.

I asked the Jangles brothers if they had any idea of how long it might take a traveler on land to reach New Orleans. They both scratched their heads indicating that they hadn't a clue. Then the older brother, Jonathan Jangles, said, "I couldn't say how long it might take you, but it would surely take a good deal longer than a White person who could freely book a passage on a steamship or a railroad car or even travel in a stage coach over land." This answer brought home for me the reality of being someone else's property and while my life so far hadn't been so bad, compared to others around me, I knew that there was miles of distinction between a slave's life and opportunities and those of a free man.

The younger brother, Beau, then decided to show me some of his dance moves that he claimed he had been rehearsing for years. To tell the truth, he was as good, or better, than any of the best dancers I'd ever seen at any of the dances, hoe downs, or sporting establishments in my part of Georgia. He did a juba with a sliding one-step move that was nothing short of spectacular and said that he had learned it from one of the best slave dancers who lived on the nearby plantation.

Then he ended his routine on his knees and described how his future act would include a scantily clad woman assistant who would throw a cape over his shoulders and lead him off the stage. His brother whispered to me that Beau had also stolen that part from the great dancer, James, owned by Mr. Brown.

The brothers, who were allowed to take their owner's boat out to go fishing on their Sunday off, said they had to return soon and thanked me again for the pie which they had eaten and complimented several times. They mentioned that if we'd ever cross paths in the future, they'd be glad to barter whatever they carried for more of that pie (since they never had any money anyway). I gave them each a copper penny which in those days could buy a man a meal and told them I'd be glad to see them again, though I could only hope to have more of the pies and was only lucky that I had that one left.

We parted company and I continued on my way with the ocean to my left; still heading to what I thought was my destination: New Orleans. I knew I'd have to pass through a number of neighboring states and a great deal of unfamiliar territory and I dreaded being exposed to strange and often times brutal slave catchers who I had no way of knowing if they could be fooled or bamboozled.

I feared the worst, but I hoped for the best. I was torn at times between going on and going back. I realized that while I didn't know what hardships lay ahead of me, I certainly did understand what waited for me if I was to head back.

Not only did the overseer, Mr. Nasty, have a good beating waiting , but my owner, Mr. Vanderbilt, who had previously treated me exceptionally well, would have lost trust in me and felt betrayed. Furthermore, I had stolen from him, taken money from my sister and if I was apprehended by the slave catchers, my owner would have to pay another expense that would probably force him to make even more of an example of my sorry self.

Considering it would be just as difficult to sneak back as it would be to continue on, I whole-heartedly decided to throw caution to the wind and continue with my plan to escape.

In the middle of all my plans and doubts, an idea came to me that I hadn't considered until that moment. I thought of my cousin, Benjamin. He was called Uncle Ben by most folks because of his prematurely gray hair and vast knowledge of rice cultivation for such a young man. Benjamin was living on a large plantation on one of the islands off the coast of the Carolinas, what was then referred to as the low country in South Carolina.

Since Ben had formerly lived with us on the plantation, and

written after he'd left, I knew that it was only a three or four days ride from where I was to there. In his letter he had described the rice plantation where he now lived and how it was so hot and humid and infested with insects, snakes and alligators that they hardly ever saw White people there. In fact, he said, that on the whole island you could count the number of White people, using just your fingers and the toes on one foot.

Because they were living on an island, their only escape would have been by swimming or boat and the alligators ruled out swimming. While building a large enough boat would take a great deal of time and stealth since few overseers that were on the island usually rode about the coast on horseback, looking out for just that sort of thing.

The brainstorm that I had, if you can call it that, somehow told me that if I could get there, my cousin, Ben, could hide me out for as long as I could stand the uncomfortable conditions. He had written that many of the people living on the island had been there for a long while, ever since they had been brought to this country in bondage. In fact, they had retained much of their African culture and could still speak some of the languages spoken in the Gambia region and Angola. Many could also weave fine baskets and beautiful cloth and fashion fish nets that were unavailable but highly desirable in any other parts of the South.

The local people referred to their island as Gullah and although I didn't know what it meant in their dialect, I knew it was where I wanted to be, at least for the time being. I wasn't sure if my newest plan made sense or nonsense, but I'd heard that you could sometimes hide best in plain sight. So I decided that between Baltimore and New Orleans my best bet might just be an island paradise off the coast of South Carolina where most White people did not want to be.

I turned my carriage around and started heading North instead of South. At my first break area to water and feed my horse, I took out the paper and pen my sister had insisted I carry and wrote a new note for my destination and signed my owner's name. I used my sister's note as an example and simply changed the ordered directions on it. While my handwriting wasn't quite as good as my sister's, I believed it was good enough to fool the slave catchers who could barely read and write themselves.

In any event, no White person would ever guess that a slave could write a note with directions on it allowing them to run away to a place they described in writing and were actually heading toward. At this point, I wasn't sure but guessed that nobody up to this point had ever run away to an island plantation that was more isolated and uncomfortable than the place they originally came from.

Because this made a backwards logic to me, I felt even more confident than any time since the beginning of my journey. I began driving the buggy with my shoulders back and sitting up proudly as if I really was ordered to report to a plantation on an island off the coast, as soon as possible, and do what the owner there told me to do as soon as I arrived.

I had inscribed on the bottom of my traveling pass that any-one who stopped me should hurry me along in the direction of said island, since my owner's brother, also a Mr. Vanderbilt, had great need of my assistance due to his illness and condition.

While I wasn't exactly telling the truth, I felt I wasn't far from it, since elements of my story were true and I could certainly remember what my story was. No matter how this played out, I felt that I had a fair chance of success as long as my current luck held out. Being the gambler that I was and sporting man at heart, I was willing to take the chance. One of the old sayings I'd heard many times as I was growing up was, "Nothing ventured, nothing gained." Because I was risking my ass, I figured, at best, I might gain a temporary freedom that, if nothing else, would make me smile when I was an old man telling youngsters, when asked, how I got so many stripes on my back. That is, of course, if I survived.

෴

I hadn't had the need to use my cover story of being the Black Tycoon for quite some time and I suddenly wondered if I would ever use it again. For the next week, I traveled toward the Carolinas. During the day I ate from whatever unattended vegetable patches I could find. At night I slept concealed in the woods. During my journey I was never stopped or even questioned by any of the people I passed on the road. As I drew closer to my departure point for crossing the water, I wondered how I would be able to cross onto the island where cousin Ben was living. It was called The Gullah Islands, a name transferred to these mainly rice producing islands.

My options, of course, were to swim, paddle in a small boat, or drive onto the ferry and pretend that I had some business there. It was too far to swim, and I didn't have a boat or know where I could find one. My third option was partly true since I intended to hide out there and I guessed that it would fall into the general category of *monkey business.*

Located not that far between Savannah and Charlotte, the ferry crossed twice daily and unbeknownst to me, nobody asked any questions about where you were going or why you boarded the ferry, as long as you had ten cents fare or in my case because I had a horse and buggy, two bits.

I had quickly devised a story to go along with my latest forged pass, but once I was on the ferry with my buggy, I realized I didn't need it since the only thing I was asked for is my fare and if it would be cash or credit. Had I known where I was going, I might have charged it to the owner of the plantation where my cousin was working. But because servants were sometimes hired out to other farms, I wasn't sure and it was probably better that I did not in any event.

When I reached into my pocket and produced a shiny quarter for the fare collector, a few of the other bonded servants noticed and I became, within a small town, among an even smaller group of people in similar circumstances, a somewhat mysterious stranger. Realizing I was the center of attention, I asked a young boy standing close to my buggy if he knew of my cousin, Ben Coon. He said he wasn't sure, but he thought he knew most everyone on the island. He then asked me if my cousin might go by any other name or what he might look like. When I described him as being prematurely grey for a man in his early twenties, the youngster said "that sounds like Uncle Ben who works on the Vanderbilt's plantation not far from the north end of the island where I live."

I asked him how to get there and he said, "Don't worry, you can't miss it; just keep going and you'll get there."

This puzzled me so I asked, "How's that?" He explained that there is only one road that goes all around the island and passes all

41

eight plantation big houses. Off this road are lanes that go toward the center of the island to the various fields and quarters where the bonded servants lived and kept their own little garden patches and facilities. But the main road was really the only road suitable for a fine carriage such as mine and the side lanes were better suited for a person on horseback, donkey or mule cart.

I thanked the young man and asked him if the folks on this island had any fun or places that they could go, to be among our people. He answered that there were no formal places like the bars and juke joints he'd heard about in Savannah, but whenever the weather was good on Saturday evenings, most of the younger people met in a field in the middle of the island and would cook outside, dance and enjoy each other's company after a long week of working in the fields and on the various plantations.

This was where they would exchange gossip and news they'd picked up from working in the main houses, along with talk of politics and how it affected us. He also mentioned that there was also a little gambling and some pot liquor that could be had; although it wasn't considered smart to get too drunk or to miss church services the next day. The reason being there were so few White people on the island and they usually only took notice if you didn't show up for work or church. And since it was felt by the island folks that the less attention the better, pretty much everyone toed the line and tried to keep things from getting worse since everyone knew things could.

I again thanked this young boy and stored this information for future reference. I asked him if he'd like to ride with me to his plantation and in that way he could show me where my cousin could be found. He said thanks but no thanks since if he got back to the farm too soon, they would only find some work for him to do and he really wanted to stop by and visit a young lady friend of his on his way home. Instead he gave me some simple directions that he said I could not get wrong even if I tried.

His directions were to go left on the road when I got off the ferry and travel four miles until I saw a large white house with six columns in front. He said if I missed it just keep going on the road and after a spell I'd be back to the same place again, since the road was one big circle around the island. "Another comedian" I thought, and wondered if, in the future, that might be a job for our people since so many young men seemed to be so good at humor.

Not long after, the ferry pulled into Gullah Island, and I thought I was in an African paradise. Not only was the island beautiful, but the people, with the exception of the sailors on the ferry, were people of color, with nary a White person in sight. The colored folk were dressed in beautiful vibrant colors and wore head wraps that I'd never seen anywhere before in my life.

I had heard from my cousin that many of our ancestral traditions from Africa were still practiced here but never in my wildest imagination would I have guessed that the women would be dressed in what could only be described as the most beautiful African tribal attire. The dresses had long flowing striped material with matching high head wraps that made the women who had extremely good posture anyway, look even taller. The men wore white shirts that fit over their heads and were vented on the sides like short tunics. Both the men and women's shoes were open at the toes and sides and were closer to what you would have thought ancient Romans might have worn than what I was used to seeing in the rest of America. All of these garments were made here.

I noticed that some of the women around the dock looked at me strangely and must have thought that I was dressed as unusual as I thought they were. Since so few White people were seen here on the island, my attire was in the immediate minority and was considered very different or peculiar to theirs. One young woman, who I thought unusually beautiful, pointed at me and laughed and said something that sounded like 'two bob concorro.' I smiled at her and later learned that what she said was in essence 'White man's clown clothes.'

Her name was Arwinda and she reminded me of my sister; strong, beautiful, independent, fearless and no nonsense. At the time I imagined all of this because I really didn't know her; but I soon would and found that my initial impression was on the money.

It took me less than an hour to drive my buggy from the dock, where the ferry landed, to the plantation where I'd been told my cousin, Ben, called home. I drove up to the front of the plantation and was instructed by one of the servants there to pull around back to a nearby stable. When I got to the stable, one of the stable hands, I guessed, asked me if I was the new driver for his owner, Mr. Vanderbilt.

I replied that I wasn't certain but that I was seeking Uncle Ben, as he was called locally. He told me I'd probably find Ben in one of the many rice fields down yonder but he wasn't sure which. He added that it would probably be easier to find him at evening meal since all the folks working on the plantation ate together in the field house reserved for the workers living on the plantation. He also instructed me where to put my horse and carriage, where the feed and water were and told me I was welcome to walk around and tour my new home or, at least, what he assumed would be my new home.

Before he left he said, "Young man since you are new here, I'll give you some valuable advice: There are only two or sometimes three White people on this plantation. Our people run this place and the way we do it is by knowing what they want and having it done before they ask. In other words", he said "we go along to get along." "In this manner we run the joint, it don't run us. Stick to the plan and you can be your own man and enjoy as much freedom as any of us have ever experienced in this new world."

I left him and began to wander the grounds which were quite extensive, wondering about what he told me and what exactly it meant in the position I was in; hiding on my owner's brother's plantation as a stowaway slave, disguised as a slave. I passed more than 100 folks working in the fields close to the main house and realized that this was only a small part of the entire property. The plantation, my former home, wasn't one quarter as large and couldn't have, from what I'd seen so far, as many as one quarter the servants and field hands that I saw right here. Also during my travels, I'd noticed the slave quarters and how differently they had been laid out and decorated.

Although my knowledge of this style was limited to what I had heard from my elders, it seemed that the servants' quarters were modeled from an African village where the small houses were laid out in a circular fashion around a large open sided roofed enclosure that served as a common space for the woman to share communal tasks such as cloth making and clothing repair, basket weaving and braiding their children's hair. The men used this space in the evenings for meetings to discuss whatever they thought interesting or important.

The men and women lived separately even when married. The women had their children with them until the boys were ten and would be considered almost grown, and the girls stayed until they had their own children or married, which usually happened after their sixteenth year. Their customs were probably unique to the island since many of them had lived here for generations and their ancestors had been brought directly here when they first reached America's shores.

In my wanderings around my new plantation, I passed the road that led in from the main road and noticed a number of people walking in who had been on the ferry with me crossing from the Carolina mainland. Among them was the beautiful girl who I had noticed laughing at me, Arwinda. She seemed to notice me as well when she passed and smiled again, although she seemed a bit tired from what I guessed had been close to a four mile walk from the ferry's dock.

That evening at the dinner hour, I finally came across my cousin, Ben. Actually, Ben found me and said that he'd heard a new driver was walking around the plantation dressed in White man's clothes and looking like a clown. I mentioned that I had a long story to tell him, but I thought it might be better later when we were alone. I also asked him why people thought I was the new driver since I didn't know anything about that particular job being available.

Ben told me that the job was available because the last driver had drowned in the ocean a while back after drinking too much and attempting to swim to the mainland. He said that the boy had rocks in his head. They hadn't told the owner what he was trying to do; only that he had drowned. He also said that the less the owner knew, the better off everyone was and sometimes you could go as long as three or four months without seeing one White person; especially if you didn't go near the Big House during spring and early summer.

We decided to take our food and walk a little distance from where everyone was eating. Ben told me that while the folks on the plantation worked together, everyone couldn't be trusted not to try to get special consideration from the boss or owner for information that might be special or important. He explained that because of his knowledge of rice cultivation, acquired from his father and grandfather, he was in a unique position as a planting and growing supervisor. This position gave him free reign to travel around the plantation fields as he desired or thought necessary. Furthermore, it allowed him to occasionally travel back to the mainland to purchase seed and fertilizer for use in the rice fields here. This position also required him to do very little hard labor. Consequently, because of his obvious intelligence and close working relationship with the boss, he was held in high esteem by the other folks who worked and were owned by the plantation.

Now that I knew what he had been up to for the last four or five years since we'd last seen each other, he asked me, "Why did they send you here? I thought you were getting along fine in Georgia driving for the owner down there and all!"

I explained my situation regarding "Mr. Nasty's" daughter, and admitted to my cousin that when I initially left I didn't have any idea where I was going except that I knew, for my own safety, I had to leave.

Ben said he understood where I was coming from but did not really get where I was going to. He said, "I heard of slaves running off to see their children or their wives and husbands on other plantations, but for a slave to run off his plantation and hide on another did not make a lot of sense."

I admitted the same, but after a month on the road and the few adventures I had encountered, I found myself heading towards Ben's place just because it was familiar.

"I'm here because I hardly know anyone any place else outside of my home plantation." My cousin said, "Your plan may sound crazy, but because of the position I'm in here, it might just work or at least until this war starts and all the Southern White men go off to fight and we can be free." He said the most important thing for me to do was not tell anyone that we were cousins. In that way, he could do many things for me on the plantation without anyone suspecting favoritism.

Also, when he went to the mainland, I would probably drive him there to get supplies since he planned to hide me in plain sight as the master's driver. He figured that when the next driver showed up, they could simply rearrange his papers and instead have him driving the rice carts that moved supplies around the extensive fields of the plantation.

I was very lucky in deciding to come here because I never realized how much clout my cousin had and how little involvement most White people had with the rice plantations on these islands. Ben said that I should call him Uncle Ben since most folks on the plantation did; and it would reinforce our story of only having been acquaintances from the past. Also, he explained to me, and it was important, the concept of possible denial. That is, if he did not know about me, he couldn't get into any trouble in the event that I did.

We both knew that helping a runaway could and would lead to a seriously bad time for anyone involved, but we also knew that if we didn't help each other no one else could be expected to. During our childhood, we had been great friends and running buddies and got into all kinds of what was called then "devilment" together. Funny as it might seem now, most of the time we got away with whatever we shouldn't have been doing.

Uncle Ben, as I now determinedly called him, said, "I love it when a plan comes together even if this is the wildest plan I've ever been involved in."

"The first thing you'll need is some new clothes if you're going to fit in here. I know just the young lady that can help you out."

He explained to me that the women on the plantation made all the clothes for the men on the grounds; and here you were expected to pay them anyway you can, that is if you weren't related or married to them.

We went back to the quarters' large eating area and Uncle Ben introduced me as the new driver from a plantation where he used to live. The introductions were mainly to men who also held important positions on the plantation and could help me during my period of readjustment. He also introduced me to a large woman who was the main cook in the quarters and explained that the cook, as far as he was concerned, was the most important person on the plantation and deserved a great deal of respect.

I gathered from the introductions that my cousin, whom I now referred to as Uncle, was also held in high regard and well respected here because of his intelligence and the importance of his position as the main grower or boss man cultivator of the rice crop. There were, of course other crops, fruits and vegetables growing on the plantation, along with nuts and flowers. But rice was the main cash crop, and African slaves knew more about planting, growing, and harvesting this particular sought after Carolina long grain rice than anyone else in the country. Because my cousin was the main man in that department, I was well connected, to say the very least.

Before we left the eating area, Ben said there was one more person that I needed to meet and then he would show me where I could sleep for the night. Tomorrow, he would bring me up to the Big House and introduce me to the owner, Mr. Vanderbilt, who I would be driving for and who would also tell me where my sleeping quarters were. I expected that would probably be where Ben was taking me anyway, but he didn't want the owner to feel that he knew what was going to happen before it happened.

The first person my cousin took me to, was the woman who would be making my new clothes. I expected a much older woman but was pleasantly surprised when my cousin brought me over to a corner of the eating area where a group of young and very beautiful women were all seated together eating and chatting at the same time.

As we approached their table Ben said, "Excuse me ladies", and they all looked up and smiled at Ben and then noticed me and seemed, in my mind, to be wondering 'who is this new Negro and why is he dressed like a White man going out to a dinner party?'

I was even more surprised when Ben said, "Arwinda, this is an old friend of mine, Ty, who has come to live on our plantation and will be working in the main house as a driver for Mr. Vanderbilt."

"He needs some clothes and he will be glad to pay you. I told him that you will give him a price."

This was the same girl who had smiled at me and laughed at my appearance when I noticed her on the ferry. This was the girl of my dreams.

After she said something to her girlfriends in a dialect that I didn't understand, that made everyone including Ben laugh, she turned to Ben and myself and said, "I'd be glad to help this young man, Uncle Ben; please send him to the center of my quarter tomorrow after ten o'clock and thank you for bringing me work."

We left after Ben thanked her and said goodnight to the other ladies and apologized for interrupting their dinner hour with business.

I was very excited to say the least. I told my cousin that I had already seen Arwinda on my way over from the mainland on and thought she was very beautiful. I asked him if he had chosen her because of that reason. He looked at me like he was studying me after not having seen me for a long period of time. He answered, "Ty, listen carefully, because this is important. Yes and no is the answer to your question. First yes, she is very beautiful and any man who isn't strange would love to have Arwinda around him doing anything; but no—that isn't the reason. I asked her to make clothing for you because she is the best seamstress on this island. Her mother, who recently passed, was the best before her and her grandmother was the best of them all. Her people are said to go back to royalty in Africa and everyone here on this island, knows it for truth because the oldest people here heard it from their grandparents who came on the first boats."

Ben went on to say, "Among our people, she is not only a princess but a warrior and before you say anything to her that you think might be sassy or offensive, be aware she could easily kill you with skills her father taught her years ago as a young girl when he was still alive. More importantly," he exclaimed, "there's a man here who you haven't met that has been waiting to marry her for the last three or four years. Because her mother was sick, Arwinda wouldn't think of matrimony and insisted on spending as much time as possible taking care of her."

"This man who's been waiting for Arwinda goes by the name of Uhuru, which means freedom in Swahili. He is one of the largest, strongest, meanest field hands you have ever laid eyes on in this life. He is originally from Barbados where it's said that he struck down a number of British soldiers who ordered him to do something he didn't feel they had authority to ask of him. Rather than let the constables put him in jail, his owner sold him to this plantation and quickly got him off the island mainly because he was such a good worker and secondly because his owner didn't want to lose the money Uhuru would bring in a sale."

"This fellow I'm talking about is not only big, strong, mean and fast, but he was the number one stick fighter in Barbados. And if you've never seen or heard of it; they put a stick in both hands and with a bunch of strange defensive dancing maneuvers, manage to beat their opponent's brains out from six or more feet away while dancing around them in circles.

Ben said, "You know we go back a long way, Ty, and I'm awfully glad to see you; but it's much too dangerous to even have people here mistakenly think that you're interested in Arwinda, especially since you'll be working in the Big House and the field people aren't too fond of the house people anyway. I also remember you as being a ladies man and the women here who aren't already married might just be susceptible to a new man's sweet talk. But take some good advice from a friend and your cousin. News travels fast even on a farm as big as this. If you say something to a girl here and travel to the other end of the plantation, by the time you get there they'll already know what you said."

I knew my cousin was right and I thanked him and admitted that Arwinda could have been the girl of my dreams but then so could many others. We both laughed but I wasn't sure how funny it really was.

"One question" I posed to my cousin. "What exactly did Arwinda say to her girlfriends that had everyone laughing?"

He said, "That's Gullah and you'll learn it if you stay here long enough. She said she saw you on the ferry and noticed you were dressed like a White man going to a funeral and now she has to make clothes for you to look like a human being. This job is not going to be easy but when I'm done, one of you girls might see a cute little African that you might want to get next to."

I laughed at this while inwardly wondering what it meant and if it was a good or bad omen related to any future I might have with Arwinda. Then just as quickly, I put it out of my mind and followed Uncle Ben to what would be my home for the next six years.

The quarters Ben led me to was a palace compared to the small house I lived in on my previous residence. I could only describe it as a garrote apartment over the stable, but it was both luxurious and private while also conveniently located above the area where I would be keeping the horse and buggy that I would be required to drive for the plantation owner and his family. This carriage house was a little more than 100 yards from the main house, and while it was located for the convenience of the owner, it was also perfect for me since none of the other people working or living on the plantation were anywhere near me unless they slept in the Big House. This afforded me close to complete privacy since the nearest slave quarters were a quarter mile away and from my window I could see White people and Black as well, having a view of the main road leading up to the Big House.

My vantage point allowed me to see who would be visiting the owner's house and put me in a unique position to have news that few others on the plantation had. Things like if a doctor was there or a rice buyer or the owner's daughter visiting home from school. This was all valuable information in the quarters and would catapult me to the top of the gossip carts even though I was the newest person here.

The next morning Ben showed up early and walked me to breakfast before he said he would take me up to the Big House for introductions to my new boss. First he said we had to get our story straight and that's what we concentrated on during our morning meal. I asked Ben how I should act when I met my new owner.

"Damned if I know. We're going to meet the boss of the plantation now, not the owner; and the boss is a free Black man who came from Boston to live here on the plantation."

"He's been here for the last thirty years, long before I got here. People say he came here because his mother was here and when his former owner set him free, he didn't know where he wanted to live but decided to be close to his mother who lived here until she died, which was also before I got here."

Ben went on to tell me that everyone called the boss "professor" because he was said to be the best educated Black man in the Carolinas. He was educated at Harvard University in Cambridge while his owner, a young man, went to school there and took him to class every day to carry his books and assist him as a man servant.

His owner, who was somewhat of a gambling man, won a great deal of money betting that his servant was smarter than the other servants held by the other White students.

Not only did the professor prove to be the most intelligent servant and win a great deal of money for his owner in contest, but when none of the other White students would bet against him, they began hiring him out by the day to prep them before exams. When his owner finally graduated from Harvard, he gave the professor his freedom and said that it was only fair since he had won enough money with him to buy twenty slaves *and* a team of horses.

The professor had been here ever since and runs the plantation like an overseer accountant. He knows everything that happens on the farm and there's no sense trying to fool him. Ben said "If he asks you a question, tell him the truth. Do remember what I said about plausible denial though because it should apply to him as well as me. Don't tell him anything that would get him in trouble. If you tell me, I'll tell him what I think he can handle and what I think he'll go along with. He and I have a very good working relationship and there isn't much I can't do here on the plantation without his help. Having said that, I think you'll get along fine with him and he's probably the one here who can help you the most when it's time to leave since he's one of the few who's also been in the North and in the outside world, off a plantation."

Ben brought me over to the Big House and ushered me into a waiting room on the first floor. All the maids and house servants spoke to him in a deferential manner and it was obvious that they felt he was one of the more important slaves working on the plantation. He instructed me to wait a minute and said he'd be right back to bring me in to meet the boss. In less than ten minutes he reappeared, "Come with me. The professor is ready for you now."

I was then ushered down a corridor and into a medium sized office where the walls were lined with books and ledgers. There was one chair empty sitting in front of a large desk, behind which sat the professor, the boss of the plantation.

He wasn't at all what I had expected, but he was undeniably impressive. When he rose to greet me, I noticed that he looked to be at least six feet, four inches tall and I would have guessed he weighed in the vicinity of four hundred pounds. Other than the spectacles he wore and his high pitched voice, he looked more like a giant wrestler than a professor. When he spoke to me, however, he sounded exactly like a white man and if it wasn't for the complexion of his skin, I would have thought he was.

I had never seen a Black man as large as him although I had seen some taller. The amount of food it must have required to become that large had to mean that he was either incredibly rich or very important. I was impressed to say the least.

He greeted me warmly and told me to please sit down and make myself comfortable. While Ben made his exit, the professor started our interview by saying, "Uncle Ben speaks very highly of you and tells me you were on the same plantation with him in Georgia a number of years ago." I nodded my agreement.

"I've come to trust his judgment over the years and I'm sure you'll do a fine job here based on his recommendation."

"Thank you." I replied.

"There are a few things, however, I'd like to explain to you that are somewhat different here than on most other plantations. These things are important because they distinguish the quality of life here as better than any other place I've been and I have experienced being chattel as well as a free Black man, in both the South and the North."

"Now before I explain what I think you need to know, I want you to understand that I realize that you are not the driver I sent for since I sent that request myself and it wasn't to your former owner, Mr. Vanderbilt's, brother in Georgia. Nevertheless, Uncle Ben said you wanted to be here and I was in a similar position myself years ago, so I won't question your motives. I can pretend ignorance as well or better than the next man and I don't see how I could get into any trouble assigning a slave to work. As far as I'm concerned, there is no law against that and if there were, I would know it."

The professor carried on, "What's different here is that I run this place. There are no slave drivers. Everyone eats well, there is no brutality, and everyone has enough clothes and is comfortably housed. Because we're on an island, there is no escape unless you can swim ten miles and in the last twenty or more years, I haven't heard of anyone being successful yet. We have a saying here: 'we go along to get along.' That means we do the work that's expected of us and we're pretty much left alone. The owner here, who is both intelligent and innovative, hired me years ago to run this farm when the only thing a free Black man could do at that time was get out of the South, if he was lucky."

"We have had people here who have run off to hide, committed suicide or have been sold because they didn't want to work. They sometimes think the grass is greener somewhere else. I've been there, it's not! What I maintain here is what I call an open door policy and that means if you want to leave, get to steppin', but don't think you can come back. Because if I have to tell the owner that someone's gone and I have to put an ad in the papers and offer a reward and then send for new help, it makes us all look bad here and increases the scrutiny on us. We don't want that and don't need it." He paused, looking at me eye to eye and continued "I understand there are lazy people among us but I find it intolerable in my position. We are a group operating in a unique setting; and as such, we need every single person to carry his own weight. If not, then the few of us who do work must carry the extra burden. That is unacceptable.

I hope you understand this well, because I spent a good deal of my life in a similar position as you and the rest of the folks here, and I don't want to make life any harder on you than it already is. However, we have rules on this farm and they must be followed.

Before I tell you what your job entails, do you have any questions so far?"

Remembering what my sister said, I squared my shoulders and asked, "Sir how would you like me to address you?"

"You can call me professor. Everyone else does."

"Professor, if you don't mind I'm curious about why a free Black man as obviously well-educated as yourself would choose to come back to the South and live on a plantation when he could live anywhere else?" His reply told me a lot about the outside world, which I could only imagine free Black people inhabited at the time.

He cocked his head at me and said, "Ty, that's a very good question that no one has ever had the courage to ask. I know that people think I came here to be close to my mother, but that was only a part of it. When I went to school with my former owner, I realized that many of our people had the intelligence and ability to compete with the White man if given the opportunity. Just like I know that you can read and write because you and Ben's former owner gave you the opportunity. But what I also learned is that in this country now, the Black man is held in such low esteem that regardless of his ability he is still considered a second class citizen and will never be given an opportunity to compete on a level playing field. Maybe that will change some day."

He continued, "Notwithstanding, a man must work for his daily bread and a job is a job. After being abused and ignored in Boston and run out of some of the poorest white neighborhoods by little White children throwing stones at me and screaming 'kill the Black giant,' I decided to return to the South and find a job where I might be able to help my people while also making a good living. So here I am, well fed and decently paid. While it may seem that I'm in the same position as the folks that are considered chattel on this plantation, the simple fact that I can leave if I wish gives me a completely different perspective. I know that I'm here because I want to be." The professor, paused, wet his lips and went on to say "Now, if I've answered your question, let me explain what your job will require of you."

He then proceeded to spell out my duties. "First, most of the time you won't be driving the owner, Mr. Vanderbilt, because he is seldom here and when he is, he only goes out at the most six times a year. His wife and daughter, on the other hand, will keep you extremely busy whenever they're here. They both love to shop and it won't be uncommon for you to take them back and forth on the ferry. Your main duties will be to drive to town where the ferry comes in and pick up various mechanical parts, seeds and fertilizer, and other supplies that I've ordered for the farm."

"Occasionally, Uncle Ben will go with you to make sure they've sent us the correct farming equipment before we haul it back here. No one knows the equipment better than Uncle Ben."

"There will also be times when you travel alone. I used to take the ride into town myself, but I've done it so many times over the years that I no longer wish to. I mention that so you'll realize when you go that everyone here knows exactly how long the trip should take you and you shouldn't feel that because you're alone you can hang around and spend a lot of time jawboning with the folks from the other plantations. I might understand five or ten minutes, or even one half an hour turnaround time, but you can't take all day. And you can't be seen as a lay about or procrastinator by anyone down there, since you represent this farm."

"When you're driving the owner's wife, Mrs. Vanderbilt, or his daughter, Miss Daisy, it's an entirely different job. Then you will be gone all day and then you will be expected to be on your best servant's behavior. By that I mean, '*Yes ma'am, No ma'am, what can I carry for you please?*' and you must be especially discreet. If any gossip comes back to this farm about whom young Miss Daisy was flirting with or who paid special attention to Mrs. Vanderbilt, you may not last long. No doubt, Uncle Ben already told you how the lines of communication on this farm, what we call the grapevine, go from the farthest field to the inner corners of this very big house and travel fast."

"If you have a girlfriend here, or on any other plantation, the less they know about your work the better you are. And they will try to get as much information from you as they can, so be guarded. At times, an innocent question can have serious and damaging consequences. Like anywhere else there are groups and clicks here that have long standing feuds and rivalries. Without telling you any stories from my own experience, 'she said, he said,' can come back to bite you on the butt. So don't be the person identified as 'he said.' Remember, you're one of the few folks living on this farm with transportation and access to a lot of information. You will be in big demand, not only because of your youth and position but because of the information that many seek to improve their own position by obtaining inside knowledge about what's going on or what's happening before it happens. Be careful. From time to time you'll hear outrageous news that's entirely false. If you repeat it, not only will most people know that you don't know jack but they will also probably know who told you and why."

"You surely understand the term 'keep your cards close to your vest'? Well, take it for gospel. In the next few months and upcoming year, you're going to hear a lot about the War Between the States that most people feel is inevitable. You'll hear the White people talk about how it's going to affect the market and what it's going to mean to cotton, sugar beets, and rice; and how badly it's going to impact the plantations in the South. They may or may not talk, in front of you, about how it will affect the chattel population of slaves down here; but then again sometimes we're close to invisible and they may. What I want to forewarn you about is that there isn't much we can do about it and to spread what you may hear among your less educated countrymen might only cause more harm than good because of the fear that it might generate."

"I'm not sure that you've ever heard the saying that goes 'The strong do what they will, while the weak suffer what they must.' That's the position our race is in and I'm afraid that it'll be quite a few years after this coming war is over before much changes for us."

"Having said all that, there are two more people that you will occasionally drive around. One is an older woman who works as a healer and lives on the next plantation, two and a half miles from here. Her name is Sellamena and she inherited the gift of healing from her ancestors in Africa. She's so good that when the White doctor on this island gets sick, they call her. Everyone on this island uses her and its common knowledge that if you are really ill, you're better off with her treatment than Dr. Abernathy's. However, there are still some of the White people here, although not many, that don't trust Black people's medicine and won't use her because they think of her as a witch doctor. I say shame on them, it's their loss."

"The other person that you will at times carry to other plantations is our beautiful young seamstress Arwinda. I've already heard that she's going to be making clothes for you, so you see here news really does travel fast. Words of caution though, when you drive Arwinda to her different jobs, try not to look too infatuated with her at least for outward appearances. She has a very jealous suitor who many suspect to be extremely violent. Between you and me, I'm not so sure he didn't have something to do with the unfortunate demise of your predecessor. The driver here that you're replacing was a young fool. He both drank and talked too much and while he was good at his job, he had a difficult time staying out of trouble and most people here wouldn't have bet he would see old age. That information is given to you because you're a friend of Ben's. Keep it under your hat, but keep it in mind so you don't get into trouble."

"I'll send a note for you every morning through my messenger boy, Jomo. If you haven't noticed it yet, there's a bell on a string in the bedroom of your quarters over the stable. He'll ring your bell and leave the note downstairs unless there's an emergency and you are needed right away. In that case, he'll ring your bell and come up and tell you what I want. There's a grandfather clock in your quarters. Remember to wind it so you can make your appointments on time. You should be ten minutes early whenever you can, and remember to keep an umbrella in your coach especially for Mrs. Vanderbilt and Miss Daisy."

The professor looked at me seriously and said, "Ty, I know you are a young man and your head is full of dreams and ideas, but if you don't mind taking some advice from a man such as me who was once as young as you; this farm isn't a bad place to be, considering all the rest. Your life is and will be what you make of it. There is no job and no labor that doesn't have honor. While we now are, as a race, held in the lowest of esteem; someday the world will realize that our labor built this country. So do your best and smile every day because it's a gift from God. If you believe in the Good Book, 'the humble and the meek will inherit the earth'. That means that someday this will all be yours so do your best and you won't have any problems here."

The last thing the professor said to me was "Spend the rest of the day cleaning your carriage and the other carriage in the stable. Tomorrow morning at six a.m., you'll hear the bell ring and you'll have your list of assignments for the day. Remember you work seven days a week, but some days you won't have much to do at all so try to keep busy and don't get into any trouble."

I left and headed back to my quarters over the stables with my head spinning. I was elated that I was in a place where, at least for the time being, I was safe. But I had escaped from being a slave on one farm to being a slave on another; and I was getting advice from a former slave who was now a free man, living on the same plantation as the slaves who he was in charge of. I wondered if 'up' was still 'up' or had I somehow wandered into another world where the old rules had shifted and the next thing I would see are White slaves working on a Black-owned plantation!

I busied myself through the day cleaning the carriages and getting my clothes put away and my quarters in order. I felt good about my new living conditions and looked forward to the meeting the next day with Arwinda so I could be measured for the new clothes she would be making for me. I reminded myself to bathe especially well and brush my hair and teeth so that if she was close to me while taking measurements, she wouldn't find me offensive.

After spending the day in my quarters and the stable below in a cleaning frenzy, I put myself to bed early that evening just after the sun went down. I anticipated being busy the following day, my first on the job in my new home, and I wanted to be refreshed and ready. I wondered if I would dream of Arwinda that night.

Just after I put my head on the pillow, it seemed I heard a bell ringing. When I opened my eyes, a small urchin boy with the largest eyes and mischievous smile peered at me from the foot of my bed. "Rise and shine Mr. Ty. I'm Jomo and the boss sent me over here to give you a list of things he wants you to take care of today."

Jomo explained that he would normally ring my bell and simply leave the list downstairs on the workbench in the stable, but the professor told him to introduce himself to the new man. Jomo said that if I had any questions about how to get anywhere, I could ask him since he was born on the island and knew everything about it and everyone here. He looked to me to be around ten years old, but I could see he was an intelligent lad by the way he carried himself and the confident way he spoke.

He surprised me by saying that he'd heard I was a friend of Uncle Ben's and because of that he was going to give me some advice, for my own good. He said that he had read my work list on his way over from the Big House and that he noticed I would be driving Arwinda to a farm a few miles from here. He wanted me to know that she was *his* girlfriend and not to get any ideas in my head. He also said that if I ran into that big dufus, Uhuru, I should tell him the same thing. He smiled again in his impish way and ran down the stairs hollering, "Sleepy head get out of bed, and if you fall back asleep you'll be in trouble deep. I'll see you tomorrow morning."

I picked up the list Jomo had left and got out of the bed and started getting myself together. My earliest appointment was to pick up Arwinda at 10:15 a.m. and carry her to a nearby plantation where she would do fittings of some sort or take measurements and then I was to bring her back here. Because of the timing involved it seemed apparent that the professor already knew that I was supposed to meet her at 10 o'clock at her quarters for my own fitting. I wondered if there was anything that went on here that he didn't know?

I heard my bell ring again and remembered that Uncle Ben said he would be coming by to show me where Arwinda's quarters were. Just as I expected he came up the stairs and said, "I came early so we could go over to the camp kitchen and have something for breakfast."

We meandered over there while Ben explained the jobs on my list and gave me directions on how to get to them. In explaining my jobs to me, Ben brought me to the realization that what I would be doing was more of a transportation facilitator or coach driver for the various people involved in the business of the plantation than an actual personal driver for the owner or his family. In fact, they were here so seldom that if all I did was drive for them, then seven or eight months out of the year I would either have nothing to do or I would have to travel with them to wherever it was they were going when they were not on the plantation.

Following breakfast I drove Ben to the female quarters where Arwinda lived and made clothing. Her housing quarters were in a beautiful tree shaded area a little more than a mile from my quarters, next to a small swift moving stream. Ben explained to me that the women on the plantation had most of the best locations for their quarters based on privacy and the fact that where the streams ran swiftly, there were less mosquitoes and bathing and washing clothes was more easily accomplished.

We found Arwinda already busy working on some garments in the main hut in the middle of her quarters with two young girls, barely in their teens, who seemed to be her apprentices. She greeted us and introduced her helpers and told me that these young ladies had already helped her to make some clothes for me. I said I was pleased that she worked so quickly but I didn't understand how she could know my size.

Arwinda smiled at me, "Mr. Ty, I've been making clothes since before I was the age of these young girls here; surely I can tell what size garments you need. Here, try this on."

She went to a rack of clothing behind her and took down a beautifully patterned African styled tunic shirt and said, "This will fit." I asked "Do you have a place where I could change?"

"Yes, you could change right here."

She then inquired, "You're not shy are you Mr. Ty?" Before I could respond, she continued somewhat straightforward,

"If you are, then I'm afraid you won't be able to bathe with the other young people here in the river on Saturday afternoons, since we all bathe naked and have no secrets from each other."

I don't remember if I blushed, but I replied, "No, I'm certainly not shy but I'm not familiar with your local customs and I didn't want to offend the young ladies or yourself."

Arwinda smiled again and appeared to be even more beautiful. "Mr. Ty, you couldn't offend us unless you said you didn't like the clothing we made for you."

With that I took my shirt off while the group watched and began to pull the beautiful tunic over my head. One of the young girls said something in the Gullah dialect that I didn't understand and they all laughed, including Ben. I looked at them quizzically as Ben translated, "They want to know how a man who obviously hasn't done one day of field work gets those muscles?"

Ben answered her, also in Creole, and when finished, she nodded her head and said, "Now I understand." Ben then told me in English that he had explained that when he and I were children on another farm, we used to run and climb and play games and that my muscles were left over from then even though I now had a soft job driving a carriage. At that moment, I decided I had to learn the local language, if I was going to be able to fit in.

The shirt I tried on was not only a perfect fit, but felt as soft as anything I had ever worn against my skin. At first I wondered if it was silk, but I knew it was cotton and even before I could ask, Arwinda said, "We made that cloth here on the farm and it's lighter and stronger than anything you can buy in the best stores in Charleston or Savannah." She said they'd had many requests from the off islanders to buy it, "but it's much too labor intensive to be profitable and also we think that because our ancestors brought the secret of the weaving process from Africa that it's too special to share with White people."

She looked at me appraising her work and said, "Mr. Ty, what do you think of your new shirt?" I said, "I'm not sure what I should say, but the shirt is beautiful, comfortable, fits perfectly and is the softest cloth that I've ever felt on my skin."

Arwinda asked if I was just saying that because I thought it was what she wanted to hear. I said "no I wouldn't exaggerate or flatter you unless it was true. In fact," I added "only this morning I'd been warned by a young man named Jomo to be careful what I said to you because you were already spoken for by him and he didn't think too kindly about any competition." Arwinda laughed and said Jomo was the closest thing she had to a boyfriend on the plantation although some others might think otherwise.

I was encouraged by what she said but pretended that it didn't register with me for the sake of both her and my cousin, Ben, who had warned me about her potentially violent suitor. I then asked her when she would be ready to leave for the plantation since I had been assigned to take her. She said to give her ten minutes to collect some material to show her customer. I asked Ben if there was any place I could take him and he thanked me but said he would walk from here and that he would see me at the evening meal.

While I waited for Arwinda, to return from her quarters, her young apprentices asked me a number of questions about where I had been before coming to this plantation, what I had seen, and had I ever been married.

Before I even had enough time to figure out what kind of story I should tell them so I wouldn't get myself in trouble, Arwinda showed up with a number of large bags and climbed into the back of my carriage. She told the girls that she had cautioned them about questioning the customers and reminded them that it also applied to customers even when they were young and handsome. I may have blushed, but I was secretly pleased that this girl of my dreams would include me in a category such as that.

I asked Arwinda if she knew the way to our destination. She nodded saying "Simply go out to the main road past your quarters and take a right away from town." She said she knew all the access roads of the island having lived here since birth and before the job of seamstress was passed down to her, she travelled with her mother and the two drivers before me when her mother was sent to other plantations to make clothes.

She also told me that once we were clear of our plantation, she would come up and sit beside me in the driver's seat but while we could still be seen by the others on our farm, it was better for her to sit in the passenger compartment.

Three or four miles down the road, Arwinda said, "Mr. Ty, pull over here." She then got out of the carriage and climbed up beside me onto the driver's seat. She explained that a woman riding in a carriage rarely rode up on the driver's seat because it wasn't considered proper decorum, but because I was new and didn't know my way around the island, it would be easier for her to show me landmarks as well as for us to talk without my looking over my shoulder or shouting.

I said I'd be glad for the company as well as any information about what was obviously going to be my new home, for however long. Arwinda said that because I spoke so well and that I was an old friend of Uncle Ben's she was sure the professor was happy that I was here and the only question would be if I was happy to be here.

I replied "the farm is beautiful and the work's not bad, they feed us well and the clothes you're making for me are the finest I've ever worn. What's not to be happy about?" I smiled.

She said what she meant was had I left anyone special where I had previously lived, and due to our position in servitude and not being free sometimes we weren't in a position to control our happiness.

I understood now what she was saying and told her that I'd left some friends and my sister at my last home; but fortunately, I hadn't been in any serious romantic involvements that would cause me regrets.

"That's good," she said. "I mean, that's good for you," trying to make it appear that she didn't personally care, while I secretly hoped that she did. I desperately wanted to ask about her other suitor, but I didn't know how without prying. The answer came to me in a flash of insight or 'out of the blue.' as we used to say. I mentioned to Arwinda that Jomo had told me that if I saw some big dufus who was also interested in her that I should repeat the same warning given me, that Jomo 'didn't want any competition'. I asked her if the fellow, Jomo referred to was her 'for real' boyfriend or fiancée. She answered "no but he thinks he is and because most folks around here are frightened of him, my social life isn't anything worth talking about."

While trying to seem uninterested on a personal level, I asked, "Not that it's any of my business and I certainly don't want to pry; but that seems strange. How does that affect you, if you don't mind me asking?'

She said that it's reduced her fun factor over the last few years to a very low number because the single men on the island are hesitant about asking her to dance at the parties and hoe downs that the folks have. "Most men don't want to be seen walking with me alone or even talking to me in any private setting."

I said, "This fellow seems to be quite serious about you? Why is it you're not interested in him? Is he that bad?"

"No. He's not bad at all, only rough around the edges." Arwinda continued, "In fact, he's tall, dark and handsome and many of the young women here would love his attention; but I'm already owned by a White man and while I can't do anything about that I'm not going to allow any Black man to think he can own me simply because he says so, even if he is big and strong enough to scare other men off."

I told Arwinda how much she sounded like and reminded me of my sister. I said I hoped things would work out for her while inwardly hoping that they wouldn't and that she and I could somehow be together. At the same time, I knew the precarious position I was in, hiding out in plain sight and knew enough after having been warned more than once, that I couldn't and shouldn't get into any trouble for my own good. I promised myself to stay away from any involvement with Arwinda but in the coming months this promise became increasingly difficult.

As we approached the plantation we had been heading for I asked her if she needed to get back into the carriage compartment. She said no that we were going right to the front of this farm's Big House and that the people working inside didn't care about any decorum that involved slaves from any other plantation. She said I could pull around back to the stable but that she would only be fifteen minutes in showing the owner's wife some fabric samples. She told me I could water and feed the horse but I didn't need to busy myself since she would be around shortly to find me.

After letting her off, I pulled around to the stable where one of the younger stable hands asked if I'd like him to tend to my stead. I said yes and thanked him and went to a basin in the corner to wash my face and stretch my legs. The young stable hand came over to me and said my horse had been taken care of and asked if I would see Jomo when I got back. He said he knew where I was from because he saw Miss Arwinda get out of my carriage and had heard the former driver had drowned.

I told him I would see Jomo the following morning and he asked me if I would mind bringing him something that he owed him. I told him as long as it wasn't too large or too dirty I wouldn't mind. He laughed and said it's only a small coin but the sooner he got it to Jomo the sooner his reputation would be intact. He'd lost a bet with Jomo at the last camp town racetrack over which horse would finish last, and he didn't have the money to pay him at the time, though he knew he soon would. I took his two penny-piece and put it in my pocket just as Arwinda came into the stables.

The stable boy said, "Good day Miss Arwinda." "Good day Franklin. How are you?"

"I'm fine Miss Arwinda and growing stronger by the day. I'll soon be ready to wrestle that big dummy that wants to marry you so don't worry; someone as pretty as yourself won't have to be stuck with somebody as big and ugly as him."

"Thank you Franklin. Remember to eat your vegetables and especially the string beans and you'll be big and tall before you know it, and then you or your friend, Jomo, can save me from the evil giant." This put the young Franklin into a spasm of laughter and I realized that even on other plantations, all the folks knew what was going on all over the island. The saying that 'it's a small world' came to my mind.

On our way back from the plantation I mentioned to Arwinda that even the small boys knew about her suitor and asked if it bothered her. She told me it used to but she's grown so used to it that she now found it quite humorous and had fun with the younger boys who vowed to save her and kept coming up with more imaginative insults for Uhuru, such as 'big dufus' or 'large dummy' or even the giant with no brain. She laughed while realizing, "The children today have no respect. I'm afraid to see what they'll be like in the future."

I asked her what amount I would owe her when she completed the task of making my clothes. She hadn't figured it out yet because she hadn't decided exactly what I needed for a wardrobe. But she said that unless I wanted to look like an old White man going to a funeral, I would probably need quite a few pieces and I could pay her whatever I could afford for her time, since everything was supplied by the plantation and the only thing she supplied was time and labor. I told her that when she finished, she could name the figure and that I felt if the rest of the clothing she was making me were anywhere near the quality of the shirt she had made already, I would be satisfied with whatever she thought was fair. She smiled at that and playfully said, "Well now you understand, don't you, that if you can't afford to pay me you'll have to be indebted to me for a period of time and do whatever I want you to do?"

I quickly replied, "I'd be more than happy if it works out that way. When the time comes we'll see what we can do."

After that exchange, we drove along for a good while, both smiling, without saying anything. I wondered what was on her mind and what she would make me do for her if I became her servant. Many different fantasies went through my head until Arwinda asked me to stop for a second and let her get back into the carriage.

"Of course, Miss Arwinda, I might just as well get used to driving you around since I might have to do this for a long time if I can't pay you." We were both amused by that and we didn't talk again until we said "goodbye" when I dropped her off at her quarters and I headed toward the stables.

At dinner that evening, I was sitting at a table with Ben when he pointed to a very large man who was walking up the middle corridor toward our table. When he drew closer, I noticed that this young man was not only large and extremely muscular, but he had a number of scars on his head, face and neck as if he'd been a gladiator or some type of professional fighter or soldier. I guessed that this fellow was none other than "Uhuru"; and when I asked Ben, he said that I was a smart lad. I noticed that he sat by himself and most of the younger men in the mess hall seemed to give him a wide berth and tried not to sit too close. I asked Ben about this and if it was my imagination.

"No," he said, "you're absolutely right. He doesn't have the best personality and is sometimes so ornery that even the young children make fun of him. Still, he can pick about as much cotton in one day as three men, and if the owner had to pay him he would probably be one of the highest paid laborers here." Having finally seen him, I decided I had been given good advice and it would definitely be in my best interest to avoid him in the future.

I continued to meet other folks working on the farm and found that, all things considered, it was a nice easy-going group, made up of equal parts young and old with a good mix of attractive young women; though nearly half were already married. The men were good natured and ran the gamut from serious to jokers, playboys and gamblers. There were only a few who were political and militant and the best known of them, Uhuru, was the one everyone avoided.

I quickly settled into my job and before long knew my way around the plantation and the rest of the island pretty well. I had made a few friends and acquired a good number of friendly acquaintances. While I hadn't yet got involved with anyone romantically, I flirted with a number of young available girls. Occasionally, I saw and spoke to Arwinda.

I drove a lot of different people to a lot of different places and finally heard from the professor that the owner and his wife would be coming for a visit from their home in Philadelphia during the next month and my schedule would be changing.

The professor said that while the owner was here I would have to be more or less on call for his wife's convenience and that I should plan on spending most of the day in my quarters over the stable so they could find me at a moment's notice. I was also told that I should dress well during the time I drove the owner's wife and daughter because they felt it was prestigious to have their driver dressed better than other drivers when they attended functions or traveled to the mainland by ferry.

It was easy for me to dress well thanks to the clothes Arwinda had made. Because she knew that I would be seen more than the average servant and the fact that I normally didn't get dirty, other than a little road dust, she went out of her way to outfit me in a splendid wardrobe of shirts, pants and matching jackets for our chilly winter evenings. I may have been fantasizing, but I also thought that she did an extra special job for me because she liked me.

When it was time to pay her and I asked how much, she jokingly told me three dollars. Keep in mind that at that time, three dollars was a princely sum that ordinarily only White people could afford. I asked her without much expression if she thought that was a fair price.

Arwinda replied, "If you were a White man in Atlanta, your wardrobe would cost you at least that."

I knew she was right and told her so, "You're absolutely correct and even though I'm just a humble servant, I intend to pay my bills and remain an honorable man."

She probably assumed that I would plead poverty and either pay her over time or, remembering our previous conversation, ask her what I could do for her to work off my debt. Instead, I took ten dollar bills out of my pocket and counted out three and handed the three to Arwinda exclaiming, "It's the best money I ever spent." I could see from her expression that she was surprised because that was a small fortune for a plantation worker or for anyone other than a free man. She asked me if I had been a gambler or a highway man before coming to the plantation.

I smiled and said "No, but if I told you what I did I'd have to kill you." I tried to keep a straight face when I said this, but I quickly broke out into a grin and so did she.

After paying Arwinda, our relationship seemed to grow better. I'm not sure if it was because she knew I had money or that she thought of me as a serious young man because I could earn and save, but whenever we passed on the plantation or the mess hall, she went out of her way to speak to me and compliment me on what I was wearing. I wasn't sure if it was because I was wearing her clothes or that I kept them clean, or that she possibly liked me. I hoped it was a combination of all three. At this point I understood the old saying, 'time passes when you're having fun'.

It was April of 1861 and the owner and his wife had arrived to spend the spring months on the plantation. When I first met them up at the ferry, they recognized their horse and carriage, but they thought I was their former driver and addressed me by his name. I explained that he had passed away and that I was the new driver who had been here now for almost a year. Mrs. Vanderbilt said that her daughter would be upset to hear the news because they seemed to get along so well. While Mr. Vanderbilt said he wasn't surprised because so many things were changing and his former driver, although he seldom saw him, didn't seem to have much in the way of common sense.

Two other things concerning changes that my new owner mentioned surprised me as well. He said that his brother in Georgia had died and some of the slaves he owned were now his property and were coming to live on this plantation. "That is unless", and this was the second surprise, "the war that had started earlier this month with shots fired on April 12th at Fort Sumter in Charleston Harbor, expanded quickly.

I knew the place he spoke of wasn't really far from where we were and I wondered why it hadn't started some place farther away, although I wouldn't know where. I told Mr. Vanderbilt I was "sorry to hear about the loss of his brother and that I had heard that he was a very good man." Of course, I didn't mention that I used to be his driver; I did realize now that he was gone, I could say almost anything and no one would know. Then I asked Mr. Vanderbilt how he felt this altercation at Fort Sumter might affect us on the plantation if it would at all.

He steadfastly began, "Although people have been talking about this coming conflict between the states, no one really knows what it will mean. I had hoped cooler heads would prevail, but there is a real movement afoot for what is called 'secession'. That would mean the United States separating into two countries; one comprised of the Northern States and the other the Southern States. If that happens, and I pray that it doesn't, Mrs. Vanderbilt and I would have to decide where we wanted to live and whether or not we could continue to own this plantation."

He went on to say "Our new president, Mr. Lincoln, seems to be an intelligent man; but, because I know so little about him, I'm not sure exactly how committed he is to his current course of action. All things considered, I'm not sure what will happen except that if this conflict escalates and drags on for more than a year, I may not be able to get down here next year from Philadelphia. That means the professor would have to continue running this place in my absence."

This information was mind expanding and raised more questions that I knew I couldn't ask my new owner, but resolved to discuss with Ben and possibly the professor. Instead I said to Mr. Vanderbilt, "Sir, I hope you enjoy your stay this year. It's a beautiful spring and the farm is bursting with crops. When people talk about politics, I get a little confused but I hope everything turns out well for you and I surely hope that you can come down here next spring and spend more time with us, Mr. Vanderbilt, sir."

~

For the next two months I seldom was called upon to drive Mr. Vanderbilt anywhere. His wife, however, often had me take her to the ferry so she could go shopping on the mainland. Mrs. Vanderbilt was a very nice lady; extremely refined and respectable, but she cautioned me to keep my eye on her daughter who she described as young and somewhat reckless.

This young college girl, who everyone called Miss Daisy, was said to be a handful whose unconventional behavior had caused more than a few gray hairs on both her parents' heads. Because she was due on the island the following week, when she returned from school for the summer, the professor called me into his office one day and explained exactly what he expected of me while she was here.

"Ty, you have to keep this crazy White woman out of trouble. She'll like you because you're young and handsome and she doesn't discriminate between the races. She drinks like a sailor and when drinking, would just as soon start a fight at a high society cotillion as in a black juke joint. And, he added, she's done both more than once so there will be no excuses accepted about being surprised by her behavior. If you expect the worst from her, you'll do a good job of protecting yourself. What I mean is, if she gets into trouble and the owners find out, you, my young friend, may find yourself demoted to the position of cleaning the hog's pen instead of driving a fine carriage."

The professor clearly wanted me to understand that if *Miss Daisy* gets into trouble, *I* get in trouble and there's nothing he can do to help me as much as he might want to. He praised my work but told me the facts straight.

"Since you've been here you've done a fine job and I've had no complaints. Everyone speaks highly of you and I'd even say that some are quite fond of you. But this assignment, although it normally only lasts a month or two, is especially important. Not only don't we want Miss Daisy to cause her family any embarrassment while she's here, but even more so, we don't want her to come to any harm even if she causes it herself."

He paused for emphasis, then continued "When she's not here, she's on her own and she's someone else's concern; but while she's here, it's all on you! And the reason is because you'll be driving her everywhere and waiting for her to bring her home safe. The only other person on the plantation she spends time with is Arwinda, who makes most of her casual clothes. Sometimes she'll take Arwinda to parties at the other farms with her because, as I said, Miss Daisy doesn't discriminate between the races and knows Arwinda is a great draw for men both Black and White. When you take them both out, be especially vigilant because the men will be attracted like bees to honey."

Now the professor lowered his tone while keeping eye to eye contact with me, "If and when, and this is not unlikely, Miss Daisy cannot walk after attending a party or cookout at one of the other plantations, you are to carry her back to your carriage and bring her home to the Big House where Arwinda will assist you in getting her into bed. Do you understand everything I just said and are we perfectly clear?"

I answered, "Yes, sir, boss." I knew from the seriousness of the professor's instructions that I could be in deep doo doo if I messed up this assignment, and it was a challenging one.

I continued with my day to day duties and tried unsuccessfully to put my upcoming responsibilities out of my head. I hadn't often been around White people who were drinking, but I knew from my experience with my own race, that while it makes some people happy and jovial, strong drink just as often made some sad and violent. And even the least educated Negro knew, at that time in the South, that to touch a White woman without her permission was asking for trouble. Furthermore, to be seen *carrying* a young White woman under the influence of alcohol might well be suicidal. Still I had my orders and I fully understood why. The only thing I didn't foresee was how my current situation that I viewed as a jackpot could easily turn out badly.

The day finally came when my assignment sheet read to pick up Miss Daisy at the ferry at 10 o'clock AM and bring her and her bags back to the plantation directly. I figured this meant no stops on the way, and I intended to do exactly what I was told. When I got to town, I was shocked by the number of suitcases Miss Daisy had. I was glad that she would be the only passenger since I needed every spare inch to carry the numerous bags and hat boxes she possessed.

Miss Daisy, who knew the horse pulling my carriage, had never seen me before and smiled at me and asked if I was the new driver and what had happened to Jeffrey, the driver before me. When I explained that he had drowned she said that was amazing since she never knew him to go swimming even when all the young people bathed together on Saturdays.

She must have known this surprised me because she flatly said, "Yes, I have gone swimming with the help on the plantation; and no, my parents don't know about it. So let's keep that to ourselves." She also said that she knew I'd probably been warned to keep an eye on her when she drinks, but told me I really didn't have to since she could handle herself just fine; much better in fact than Jeffrey, whom she speculated must have been drinking before he drowned. She said that they had often had a few nips together and after a few, Jeffrey often thought he could do things he wasn't capable of. I got the impression that she was implying something scandalous but knew better than to pursue it. I didn't want to give her any wrong impression of me.

Miss Daisy was tall, thin, blond, and built very well for a White girl. She was dressed casually, but her clothes all seemed to be a bit too tight and revealing, compared to what was normally worn in polite society. At the same time, I'd seen White women in dance halls, low class barrooms and gin mills who were scandalously dressed. I would describe Miss Daisy's attire as just short of that but leaning in that direction.

She told me she liked my shirt and guessed that Arwinda must have made it for me because it fit me so well. She went on to say that if she could bring Arwinda back East to school with her, she could make a fortune making clothes for her school mates who can't get anything nearly as nice as the clothes Arwinda makes for her. She told me her only complaint with Arwinda's clothes was that she preferred them to fit tighter. Miss Daisy said, "Don't you agree that a girl should show off what she has before she settles down?" she paused and lifted her chin, as an actress would, adding "because once she's married *it's over.*"

I didn't really know how I should answer that tricky question, so I just said, "If that's what you and the young ladies at school think, then I'm sure you're right."

Miss Daisy said, "Ty? That is your name right?"

"Yes, Miss Daisy."

"You don't have to agree with anything I say. I'm well aware that you and your people are just as smart and have as many different opinions as anyone else, including White people. You'll find that what's said and done between us will go no further and if I ever inherit this plantation, you and your people will be free the very next day. And then you'll *really* have to work because I'll expect you to pay rent if you still want to live here, for I intend to turn this plantation into a resort for Northerners wishing to escape the harsh winters."

I'd never heard anything like that before but it sounded good as well as futuristic and I liked the way she thought. I wondered if all the young White people had as many strange ideas as her and I wondered if they learned them in college or they brought them to school and polished them.

I said, "Miss Daisy, I like the way you think and I'll remember what you said. If you ever do open that resort on the plantation and I'm a free man, I'd be glad to work for you as a driver since you'll probably still need someone to pick up your guests at the ferry. In that way I could earn my rent doing something I'm already good at."

She spoke kindly back to me, "Ty, we do think alike, and I'm sure that when you're a free man, you'll be good at many things and I'd be lucky to have you work for me." On that note, we became fast friends and I think we had mutual respect for each other's intelligence and opinions. However, I still intended to keep a sharp eye on her when she was drinking, realizing it was early in the day and she probably hadn't had any nips yet.

The only other thing Miss Daisy asked about during our ride from the ferry was how Arwinda was doing and if she had married the big oaf or had she managed to poison him? When I told her Arwinda wasn't married yet, she said to me, "Well, Ty, you still have a chance."

I inquired as to why she would say that. She came back with,

"You've seen Arwinda haven't you? And I can see that you're young and handsome and must have a good education since you speak so well. I would guess that unless you were already married or you liked boys, you would automatically be attracted to Arwinda. And since I don't think you're a man who prefers other men's company and you don't wear a wedding ring, what's not to like?"

"Of course that large field hand, with the African name that I can never pronounce, does look dangerous; but I doubt Arwinda could be happy with him because his manners and conversation are a great deal lacking. I've spoken to him in the past and believe me when I was drinking, I've had better conversations with a lamp post. And it seems to me that once you're past the passion, which doesn't take long, the most important part of being together is being able to communicate with each other."

I knew she was right but I still failed to see how I could get involved with the girl of my dreams after having been warned about a dangerous giant of a man who felt she belonged to him. Of course, I had feelings for her, but I wasn't sure they were mutual, and I was even less sure what I could do about it if they were. Although Miss Daisy didn't present any problems for me in the next few weeks, I kept a sharp eye on her whenever I drove her anyplace, especially when it was of a social nature and I thought drinking might be involved.

On a number of occasions, Arwinda accompanied Miss Daisy, and while I was glad to see her, I tried to pretend it was just another assignment for me and projected what I hoped was my best professional demeanor.

Things seemed to be going along smoothly until early one evening after dropping off Miss Daisy at the Big House and going home for the night, I heard my bell ring. Certain that it wasn't yet morning, I got out of bed, and saw Jomo come up the stairs breathing like he'd run a distance. He called to me, "Come quick Mr. Ty. Arwinda needs your help. Bring your carriage."

This request was highly unusual because all my assignments came from the professor, but it seemed both legitimate and important having been delivered by Jomo. I asked Jomo what happened and he said he didn't know "but I considered it an emergency because Arwinda had sent a young girl asking me to fetch you." I quickly went down to the stable and hitched up the gray mare onto the carriage and was at Arwinda's door in less than twenty minutes.

Arwinda met me at the door and told me to keep my voice down since the less people who knew what we were doing the better off we'd both be. When I entered her quarters, for the first time, I was impressed with what I thought was the cleanest and most opulent small house I had ever seen in slave quarters. It was only two small rooms but the floors were covered with animal skin rugs and the walls were draped with cloth and fabrics. There were beautiful African art pictures and sculptures and the furniture was polished hardwood that while obviously handcrafted, would have been welcome in the richest White owned homes.

Arwinda motioned for me to come to her bedroom door and put

a finger to her lips, directing me to keep silent. It was a wise thing for her to do because when I looked into the room and saw who was there, I nearly screamed or would have. Miss Daisy was lying on her bed unconscious and barely dressed with only a light shift covering her. The shift, a type of garment I would imagine White women slept in on hot summer evenings. Her foot was bandaged and she seemed to be sweating as if she had a fever.

I'm sure I gasped when I saw her but I managed to keep my voice low and asked Arwinda what happened. I told her I had just dropped Miss Daisy off at the Big House not four hours ago. She said she didn't know what happened since then, but the snake hunter who was called "Sweets" had found her unconscious on the beach about an hour ago and brought her here. While Arwinda was undressing Miss Daisy for bed, thinking her unconscious state was from too much drinking, she noticed something stuck in the bottom of her red, swollen and possibly infected foot. Knowing her history of drinking and guessing that she might have gone for a walk on the beach without telling anyone, Arwinda thought Miss Daisy had probably removed her shoes and stepped on a poisonous sea urchin. She said she called me so we could take her to Sellamena, the healer, who lived on the next plantation a few miles away.

Because the professor had given Arwinda pretty much the same responsibility as me in looking out for Miss Daisy, we were in this together. Arwinda considered Miss Daisy a friend and she wanted to protect her reputation by not involving the only White doctor on the island. She also figured if Miss Daisy's parents didn't know, they wouldn't worry.

Arwinda, finding the surroundings absent of nosy neighbors, instructed me to carry Miss Daisy out to the carriage. She said she'd come along to direct me to Sellamena's quarters and to explain what was necessary.

I appreciated the company. Even though we were on an island where most folks were safe and unmolested while traveling, during this time in the South, a Black man traveling with a barely dressed unconscious White woman was actually begging to be hung. And the truth about it is no one would have been surprised if I was hung, only if I wasn't. While we were heading for Sellamena's, I asked

Arwinda about this snake hunter who had found Miss Daisy. I hadn't heard of him and certainly had never met him.

"Oh," she said, "he's called Sweets but he has an African name that only the professor, Sellamena and the Dogan people in Mali know. You may never see him because he lives in the forest on the plantation and hunts and cooks for himself. He's as dark as the night and doesn't make a sound when he moves through the bush. I've only seen him a couple of times myself and I've been here my whole life. He used to leave food for my mother in the middle of the night."

"Once when I was a small girl I came across him late one night, when I was going out to the bathroom. He moved so quietly and he was so dark that he appeared to be more of a shadow than anything else. When I told my mother the next day that I thought I had seen a duppy or a boogie man last night, she asked me if he had put his finger across his lips so I would keep quiet. When I said yes, she said 'don't worry little bird; he is our friend who hunts the snakes at night. As long as he's here, you won't see a snake and you don't have to fear the darkness because he is protecting us."

Awinda continued, "My mother spoke of him as a great warrior and said only a fool would wander around here after dark with bad intentions. My mother said that even the bad news rednecks that used to live on this island got into their houses after dark and prayed not to meet him in the forest. The White people fear that he was a cannibal in Africa, but we know better and know that he is our friend."

"I was told that he got here before I was born and that for whatever reason he couldn't speak English. The professor, who learned a number of African dialects, hired him to rid our plantation of snakes, which at one time, infested the island and caused everyone living here to be fearful. You may not have noticed the snakes because there are so few now. The snake man has pet mongoose that look like little weasels that will kill the largest, most poisonous snakes in a flash. They have nearly rid the whole island of the deadly snakes, but because there are now so few snakes, the mongoose are beginning to eat chickens and eggs forcing us to put strong doors on the hen houses."

As though reading my mind, she added "In case you're wondering why he's called Sweets, it's because he loves sweet pastry and I believe that was his connection to my mother. She used to bake sweet pies and desserts and leave some out for him."

"There is one other thing which will help you understand just how much this man is respected here" she said, lowering her voice almost reverently, "Early one evening four years ago when Sweets was hunting snakes near the men's quarters, where Uhuru lives, he motioned for Uhuru to keep quiet by putting his finger across his lips. Uhuru waved him off and continued to talk loudly about whatever political tirade he was on that evening. The snake man walked across the quarters to a far corner and pulled up a spear that was stuck in the ground. He hurled it the far distance across the grounds in the middle of the men's quarters into Uhuru's front door where Uhuru was standing at the time. Witnesses knew he could have killed Uhuru had he wanted to, instead Sweets pointed from his eyes to Uhuru's, leaving no doubt to any observer that Sweets would be watching every move he made. And with that Sweets stepped back into the forest where he disappeared."

"While Uhuru didn't utter a word, the amazement on his face said everything as he stared at the spear stuck in his door and it was clear to the other men in his quarters as well, that he well understood the message that had been delivered. And to this day there's still a deep hole in the middle of that door, right about eye level. No one on this plantation, or on the island, wants to run afoul of Sweets and that includes Uhuru who gives him plenty of room when he passes, although he's very seldom seen." After being on this plantation for a while, I thought I knew everything that was going on. Little did I realize that there was much that I didn't know.

In less than one half an hour, we pulled up in front of what I was told was Sellamena's house. I thought she would be very old, but she was nothing like I expected. She opened her door as soon as we drove up. She came out to us and said, "Bring the White woman into my house." While I was wondering how she knew, Arwinda whispered to me that Sellamena had the *gift of sight* which meant that the healer could see both into the future and the past.

I'd heard of such people and while I didn't truly believe in the occult, I knew better than not to believe. While growing up I'd heard so many stories of old women with *the gift* that I knew there was something to it, I simply resolved to keep an open mind. I noticed that one of Sellamena's eyes was cloudy and I had heard this was the characteristic that most fortune tellers shared. Unfortunately, I had never met one, so I had no real experience to speak of or comparison to draw from. She looked at me and said, "I know you Ty Coon and you'll soon believe in me as much as I believe in you." I had no idea how she knew my name and I'm sure I hadn't called myself by that name since I reached this island.

When I carried Miss Daisy inside, Sellamena instructed me to lay her down on a litter in the front room of her house. This room reminded me of a cross between a hospital room with shelves of jars and medicines, and a fortune teller's parlor with charts of stars and what I imagined to be witch doctor masks and strange sculptures everywhere else.

After examining Miss Daisy's foot, feeling her forehead, and looking in her mouth, Sellamena said, "This woman is very sick but she also has many troubling problems on her mind." She then said, "I can cure her sickness, but only her friends can help with her troubles. I'll get her some medicine." She then left the room through a curtain, when pulled aside I could see her going through a passageway.

Arwinda whispered to me, "Ty, she knows you from the spirit world and you must put a coin in her hand when we leave. It doesn't matter how much the coin is, it's merely a sign of respect in her tradition." I agreed and said I would. Lucky for me I had one coin; my lucky two bit piece in my pant pocket.

When Sellamena came back into the room, she handed me a glass filled with a warm yellowish, foul smelling liquid. I could have sworn it was urine but because of the strange situation, I couldn't be sure and didn't want to say anything. She turned Miss Daisy over on her stomach, put an old cloth under her foot and instructed me to pour the liquid over the bottom of Miss Daisy's foot where the infection seemed to be. I hesitated because I didn't want to do it, but I knew I had to. So I quickly poured the contents of the glass over the sole of her foot. When I did this it seemed like smoke rose up out of the site of infection and we watched a small white sliver of something that looked like a bone with a barb on the end come up to the surface. Sellamena put her face inches from Miss Daisy's foot and with a pair of tweezers removed the bone spur. She then wrapped it into the cloth and threw it into a fire pit that was burning in her chimney. She said a few words in a dialect that I didn't understand, then turned to me and said, "Thank you Ty. Some of my medicine works better when the one who administers it has a stake in the outcome."

I certainly did have a lot at stake, my ass in fact, but again I didn't know how Sellamena could know that. She looked at me like I was a child and said, "I know many things; and you will soon believe even if you don't already." Before I could say anything else, Miss Daisy woke up and looked at Arwinda and asked, "What am I doing here Arwinda?"

"You fell asleep on the beach and got something stuck in your foot so we decided to bring you here to our people's doctor so your mother and father wouldn't worry." Miss Daisy looked like she wanted to cry, but instead she said sincerely, "Thank you Arwinda and you too Ty. You're probably the two best friends I have in the world even though there are so many people I know who would call themselves friends."

She explained what happened, "When I got home earlier, I was a little depressed and I started drinking and decided I was going for a walk. I don't remember much of anything after that, but I'm sure if it wasn't for you two I might have done something stupid that no doubt could have ended badly."

Sellamena put a small bandage on Miss Daisy's foot and said, "Girl, there are many people that love you and you have to take better care of yourself. So be careful and remember that you have friends and family here that can help. All you need to do is ask; that's what we're here for. We are your people and with us behind you, you're never alone."

Miss Daisy got a little teary eyed and said, "Thank you Auntie, I'll remember." In a matter of minutes Miss Daisy got on her feet and was steady enough to leave.

Before we went out, I put my lucky two bit piece in Sellamena's hand and thanked her for her time and assistance. Without even looking at the coin, Sellamena softly said to me, "Ty, no one has ever given me as much money as you for my work--even the White people I've cured of much more serious ailments." She went on to say, "I know this is your lucky coin; and I'll return it on your wedding day, which won't be too long after the White man's war."

I returned a bewildered look at Sellamena and said, "Oh really, and do you know who exactly it is that I'll be marrying?" "Yes, Ty, we both know; and don't worry about the big stupid one who is your competition. He'll be gone soon."

We left and I was thinking about Sellamena's predictions and the part she had said about '*if I didn't believe her now I would soon*'. She had been right about my name, my lucky coin, and my desire to be with Arwinda. Could she be right about my competition, the war, and my upcoming marriage?

I asked Arwinda what she felt about Sellamena's accuracy in predictions. Arwinda said she'd never been wrong and because of that, most people on the plantation asked her to name their children. Arwinda had said, her own name, meaning *the little bird*, had in fact been chosen by Sellamena and it was spot on for what she grew to feel.

I asked Arwinda, "If it's not too personal, what do you mean?" She answered that ever since she could remember, she felt like a *little bird* and always wanted to fly away. And although she didn't know where she wanted to go, she knew she wanted to fly away somewhere. I asked if she'd heard what Sellamena had predicted for me, and Arwinda said, "No, but she's never been wrong." She then told me that even before I walked into Sellamena's house that evening, Sellamena had told her that she didn't know it yet, but the man she was with would be a very wealthy man someday soon; richer, in fact, than most White people." Arwinda again added, "She's never wrong."

We brought Miss Daisy home safely and Arwinda got her tucked into bed. When I returned Arwinda to her quarters, she said to me, "Ty, I can't thank you enough. Sellamena says she's watching you and that's the same as being born under a good sign." She went on to say "We've made a good team in this little adventure tonight and done a good thing as well. Be careful, Ty, you're a rising star on this plantation and the island and I'd really like to see you get as rich as Sellamena says you will. You know people here, like anywhere else, are jealous of those who do well. So just be careful." While I was flattered and encouraged, I didn't want Arwinda to know, so I mused, "I didn't know you cared." She looked at me funny and replied, "I know that you know that I know that you know. Good night and thank you again."

I drove home with visions of sugar plums dancing in my head, imagining that I really might have a chance with the girl of my dreams as I pondered the healer's vision. As I was brushing down the mare after unharnessing him from the carriage, I noticed a shadow flit by the open door of the stable. So few people were out at this hour of night, I wondered if it was my imagination or if the snake man, I had only just heard about tonight, was somewhere outside looking out for me and the others sleeping peacefully on the plantation.

News of the war's escalation drifted onto the plantation from time to time. We knew that we were the last ones to get the news because of our isolation here. There were a few Black sailors that worked on a rotating shift on the ferry to the mainland and folks on the island pretty much depended on them for our information about important news concerning the rest of the country. On my trips to town and the ferry dock, I was lucky if I could manage a nod or a hello from any of these black sailors. But whenever I drove Arwinda into town to pick up thread or lace or something she needed, these same sailors turned into talking machines like old women. They would gladly tell her news of what they heard in their travels and openly shared information relayed to them by the few people who could read newspapers. In this fashion, we got most of our news and information.

Occasionally, someone visiting or returning to the plantation would bring a newspaper with them from Atlanta or Charleston. Then as soon as it was discarded, or sometimes even before, it would circulate among those of us on the plantation who could read, and discussed to no end. While our initial interest was which of our neighbors had gone off to join the war efforts by joining the Confederate forces; our underlying interest was, of course, how we would ultimately be affected.

We considered ourselves fortunate because many of the Southern gentlemen slave owners brought their servants with them to the war; and either had them assist by carrying their burdens or, in some cases, fight right along beside them. Because our owner was elderly and had only one daughter, we knew none of our young men would be drafted by circumstances beyond their control. While we didn't fully understand the total implications of what this war would change or mean, most of us felt that helping the Southern war effort would only keep us in bondage. Still, there were some few who had particular relationships with their owners and felt that their best interest was so closely intertwined with their owners that they should and did go along with them to fight the Union army. Amazing and as incredible as that may seem, they may have thought that this act of loyalty could lead to their own freedom, especially if the South won the war and succeeded in becoming an independent country. There were very few of our people, at that time, who knew the difference between the size of the North and the South; and even fewer realized the economic differences that would ultimately affect the outcome. We had already heard of battles in the South where the slaves had left the nearby plantations and ran off to closely follow the Union Army. They were in this fashion, at least temporarily, free, since most of the slave catchers were already enlisted in the Confederate Army or at least trying to avoid the Union Army. A short while later, President Lincoln's Emancipation Proclamation deemed these folks living in areas at war with the Union, officially free, even though the Southern states didn't recognize Lincoln's authority because they had already seceded from the Union.

As the war raged on and more and more soldiers died, yet the event that affected me most personally was the arrival of my sister and a few others from my former home. On the morning of their arrival to our plantation, I received an assignment from the professor that said to bring the large carriage to the ferry and transport two or three people back to the farm. He didn't say who they were, but I was instructed to bring a sign, *Vanderbilt Farm*, and thus they would find me. When I parked my rig I went over to the dock where a small crowd of people were gathering after departing the ferry. You can imagine my surprise when my sister approached and hugged me and cried, "Tyronius, I thought I'd never see you again!"

I was so overjoyed that I could hardly speak. I said, "It's a long story and I'm truly glad to see you as well. I heard people were coming here from Mr. Vanderbilt's farm, but I never guessed it would be you."

She said much the same thing; that she knew she was coming here and she knew that our cousin, Ben, was here, but never guessed that this would have been my destination when I left. My sister expressed her fear that I had been captured by slave catchers and that my former overseer, Mr. Nasty, had told them to sell me to another plantation far away. She told me that ever since my former owner had died, Mr. Nasty had become even more brutal and ruled the plantation with a whip in his hand, even though it had never been necessary in the past. Mr. Nasty vowed to make an example of me if I was ever apprehended.

My sister thought one of the reasons she and Derniere, another slave who was sent here with her, had been shipped away was because they reminded the overseer of me. I could see why my sister would provoke hostility, but the only thing I could think of as far as the other woman, Derniere, was concerned was that she was so much better looking and more refined than his own daughter that this somehow also provoked his resentment and rage. Although being my sister's friend alone may have made him think that she also knew about his daughter's indiscretions.

I quickly gathered their luggage, put them in the carriage and set out for the plantation. I explained en route that they'd like it here and all the differences between the farm they had been on and the one they were going to. I told them how well Cousin Ben was doing and how and why no one on this plantation knew we were related. I told them about the boss, also known as the professor, and explained that he was a free Black man who they would soon meet upon our arrival. I assured them that he would be glad to meet them and would treat them very well. I also told them about Arwinda, Miss Daisy, and the owners, who were seldom present, but here now during the spring and early summer months. I also explained that although we were on an island and it seemed far removed from the rest of the world, it was really quite a cosmopolitan place and there was quite a lot going on.

My sister laughed and said, "That must mean that you've met a nice lady."

"It's not what you think." I hastily replied.

"Tyronius", she said, shaking her head "how could you know what I think? I just got here; give me a few days and I'll figure it out."

～

When I got to the plantation, I brought them directly to the professor in the Big House. Because I didn't know what quarters they would be staying in, I figured he could tell me while I introduced the ladies. What I hadn't expected was Ben was there talking to the boss and he jumped up and hugged my sister when he saw her. He then turned to Derniere and said, "Honey, I remember you as a little girl when I left ten years ago. You're even more beautiful now. People call you 'Dee', am I right? And how is your grandmother, Connie? Is she still feisty as ever?"

Derniere said her grandmother was fine, just moving slower, and not quite as feisty as she used to be. Then she asked Ben, "How is it that your hair has turned so gray? You're not too much older than me and you don't look like you're worried about much?"

Ben said, "God only knows about my hair; but I don't worry except about these crops. I hope you like my hair because you'll be seeing a lot of me now that you're here."

Ben then introduced both ladies to the professor. He first turned to my sister and said, "This lady, my cousin, who everyone called 'Sis', is the woman I told you about that can help you with book-keeping and your ledgers. She knows accounting and is a whiz at keeping track of money and numbers. She can do numbers in her head that most people would need an adding machine for.

The professor got up and shook hands with my sister and said, "I'm proud to meet you, Sis. I've heard about you and I must say meeting you in person is far more impressive." I thought the fact that she was very tall and extremely beautiful may have something to do with it, but I knew her knowledge of accounting would be a great asset to the professor and that he could use some help running the financial aspects of the plantation.

It dawned on me that if Arwinda was here right now, we would probably have the three most beautiful women on the plantation and the two most important men along with me in the same room. I had

THE FIRST BLACK TYCOON

purposely left out the White people, but in my world that wasn't difficult. And in my world also, I was predicted to soon become very rich; so I felt, at least a little like I might soon belong in this somewhat exclusive group.

The professor announced, "If you two ladies don't mind sharing a small house for now, I'll have Ty take you over to Arwinda's compound where we have a small two bedroom available. The ladies there will show you where we eat. Tomorrow at 10 o'clock, I'd like you to both come by here so we can discuss work assignments." The girls thanked him and said goodbye to Ben, who seemed infatuated with Derniere. I then helped them into my carriage and delivered them over to their new dwelling.

Arwinda was sitting in the center quadrant of her village square and stood up when I arrived with my sister and Derniere. She walked over to the carriage curiously. As I helped the girls down, Arwinda spoke a welcoming gesture in an African dialect that I didn't recognize. To my surprise, the girls responded in the same dialect. I wondered what I was doing while the women in my former plantation were learning so much. I guessed I was gambling, sleeping late, or gallivanting; but I couldn't really decide what.

Arwinda said, "You must be Ty's sister. There's a strong family resemblance."

"Yes I am," Sis said, "and you must be the girl that Ty was thinking about when he told me 'it's not what you think.'"

"That's possible, I'm sure; you see outside of the fortune teller saying we would be married, we have no formal relationship other than a purely professional one. By that I mean, I make his clothes and he drives me to my distant appointments."

"That's a good start. I'm Sis and my friend here is Dee. We were told that Arwinda would show us our new home and you must be the *little bird* of our ancestors' legends."

I could see that Arwinda was pleased and surprised that my sister was familiar with the ancestral legends of our people and I was even more so because I certainly didn't know them myself, though my sister had tried to teach me after our parents were gone. My sister said, "Arwinda, I noticed Ty's fine clothing and can see you are an extremely talented tailor. If you ever have time to make some clothes for me, I'd be glad to pay you whatever the cost. I don't think I've ever seen a shirt made as well as the one Ty is wearing."

"I will make time soon," replied Arwinda, "but first let me show you both to your new home. It's both clean and furnished as the women in this quarter feel it's the least we can do for our new neighbors and extended family."

"Ty, please leave Sis and Dee's bags at the corner house past my quarters."

I did as I was told and bid all the ladies good day. I knew from experience that when women start talking, a man should get walking; or, in my case, driving my carriage to the stable or my next assignment. I didn't have anything else on my assignment sheet for that day, so I hung around the stable and cleaned all of the carriages until they shined like new money.

That evening at supper, Uncle Ben asked me what I knew about Derniere. I said not much but she's always been a very smart girl and seems to get more beautiful every year. I said she's four or five years younger than my sister, but they've been friends for years and Sis used to take care of her whenever her grandmother was ill.

Ben, waving a hand impatiently, said, "I know all that, that isn't what I mean. Does she have a boyfriend? Is she spoken for?" I said I didn't think so but I'd been gone for a while so I really didn't know. I asked "Why don't you ask her?" He looked at me in disgust, "I guess I'll have to handle this myself."

I put myself to bed early that night happy that I was reunited with my sister and friends and felt that I was blessed to be in a position where although I wasn't a free man, I was surrounded by many things that even a free man would envy. When things are going good, I like to caution myself to be alert and look out for the bad. I said my prayers and hoped for the best, but the very next day my premonition would show up to haunt me.

Jomo showed up early, rang my bell and came right up the stairs to my quarters to question me about the new woman on the plantation. He said, "Hey sleepy head. I need some information and I don't want you to play dumb like you usually do. What's up with that beautiful girl, Dee, who's living in that house with your sister?"

"Yeah, I know it's your sister and thank heaven she doesn't look anything like you. She's a fox but her little roommate is just my speed and just what I need. Does she like flowers or should I try candy? Can you help a young brother out with some inside information, or are you just as useless as a donkey on roller skates?"

"Jomo, I'd like to help you, but I'm not sure she would want a man younger than herself."

"Younger, older," he said, "age is just a number and the important thing is if we have fun together; and I guarantee that Dee and me could stay out dancing till the cows come home. Can you dig it?"

I wasn't sure what he meant or what I was supposed to dig if anything, so I asked, "What makes you think she wants to go dancing with you?"

Jomo said, "Where did you grow up anyway, in a string bean patch? All fine women want to go dancing so they can show off their clothes. Boy, you are as dumb as a bag full of hammers. You better get sly before love passes you by."

"And you ask, why me? I ask you, why not me? And if not me, who? And if not now, when? Everybody wants to be with somebody; and most girls want to be with Jomo because I've got it going on."

This child talked so fast it sounded like someone rapping on a door. The last thing I heard Jomo sputter as he went down the stairs was, "Why can't colored folk help each other? The White man helps each other and they'll probably get to the moon before we get off this little island. Smarten up Mr. Ty. You need to help me out now so I'll take care of you when you're old, you big dummy."

I called back to him, "Good luck, Jomo, you're on your own."
"Thanks a lot. You're about as useful as a one legged man in an ass kicking contest," and with that he was gone.

I picked up his note and saw that my first assignment for the day was to pick up my sister and Dee early enough to bring them over to the professor for a ten o'clock meeting. I started getting ready.

When I pulled up at 9:30 AM, the women were sitting with Arwinda in the shaded area of the quarter's center. They seemed to be getting along like old time pals, laughing and joking and having fun with one of Arwinda's young apprentices. They all rose and as I helped the two ladies into my carriage, Arwinda smiled. "My life has just got richer because of my two new friends. Your sister and Dee are precious. We have so much in common and so much to talk about that I'm not sure I'll have time to make clothes."

I said, "I thought all women never ran out of things to talk about?"

"No Ty," she said, "some women never have anything to talk about because they have no imagination and no sense of humor. But your sister and Derniere could do a comedy routine on stage. They have more stories than the library in Savannah and you're in a lot of them. I'll see you later", and looking over her shoulder, smiled back at me, saying "I might have some questions later for you about your youth."

I bid goodbye to Arwinda and wished her a pleasant day and wondered if my sister living here now was a good omen. I would certainly be seeing more of the woman of my dreams now that my sister and Dee were also living nearby.

I had barely got one eighth of a mile down the road when a large burly giant of a man stepped out of the forest and grabbed my horse by the bridle just above his bit. I knew immediately who it was but was having a difficult time understanding why he was holding my horse and what he wanted with me. I would soon find out.

I said, "Turn my horse loose young man. The way you're pulling on his bridle is painful."

He roared, "Driver, my name is Uhuru and what I do to you may also be painful. You need to worry about yourself and not this old bag of bones." In his other hand, he held two sticks that were both the same length and evenly rounded. I had no doubt that these were his fighting sticks that he mastered and used in the West Indies. I noticed his English was lilted with a Caribbean accent, but what I focused on more was that my horse was bending his head over to the side so that the bit didn't bite into the corner of his mouth.

When I demanded that he turn my stead loose, Uhuru raised the sticks up in his other hand as if he were preparing to strike the horse. I couldn't tolerate anyone being cruel to an animal and especially a fine animal that I was responsible for. I instinctively pulled my buggy whip out of its holder and lashed the tip onto the back of his hand holding the sticks. He screamed, dropped them both, and started toward me where I was still sitting in the driver's seat. This time I lashed him across his face and he screamed, saying "It's not enough that you spend too much time sniffing around my woman, but now you insult me with your puny buggy whip. I'll teach you a lesson you skinny hackney driver, and you won't soon forget it!"

I'd grown up with a buggy whip in my hand; and, while I seldom if ever used it on my horses, I could crack it an inch from their ear to make them speed up or hit a horsefly in mid-air when I wanted to. I knew this giant was dangerous and I could see that he was working himself into a rage that could surely lead to a bad beating for me. I was having no part of it. My next lash caught him on his eyelid and while I could have easily put his eye out, I thought this might stop him.

It did. He bent over and put his hand over his eye while mumbling curses that had I been a West Indian would probably have insulted me or hurt my feelings. What I hadn't noticed while all this was happening was that my sister and Derniere had climbed out of the carriage and now quickly approached Uhuru with each of them holding a blade in their hand. My sister held a sugar cane knife with a short curved blade that she placed on Uhuru's neck while her girlfriend went to his other side and pressed a straight razor against his private parts. My sister stated, "Your name means freedom in Swahili, and I'll free you from this world if you mess with my brother again." Derniere spoke into his ear loud enough for me to hear, saying "You'll meet your ancestors as a girl if you bother my friend again; and if I'm living, you're dying, you black-eye-pea-eating piece of shit."

From the way I saw him trembling, I knew he was scared. Not only was he scared, but I was scared because it was abundantly clear that everyone there knew that these ladies, in spite of their appearance, meant business and I didn't want to see a great deal of blood or have to bury a giant Negro. With beads of sweat gleaming on his brow Uhuru said, almost politely, "I understand and I apologize. I had no idea the driver had family here and I only wanted him to stay away from my woman."

Derniere said, "Remember one thing, Mr. Freedom, we are all slaves here and Arwinda doesn't belong to you. In fact, you don't even own your own big dumb ass so be very careful what you say and be even more careful what you do or you'll be looking for a large dress to wear around. Now get to stepping."

I had no idea that little Miss Dee was so dangerous, but I knew now why my sister liked her so much; and I felt good that these ladies, whether on their own or with each other, were safe in any situation. Uhuru limped off into the forest holding his hand on his eye. I wasn't positive, but I really didn't think I'd be hearing from him anytime soon.

When I dropped the girls off at the Big House, it was only two minutes past ten and I realized that whole altercation couldn't have taken more than five minutes. I said goodbye to the girls and thanks for the back-up. They told me it was nothing but a little fun and they could whip that gorilla's ass even if he had his friends with him. I didn't say so but from what I'd seen, I knew they probably could. I knew my sister was a great athlete when we were younger, but I never realized until this morning that she and her friends were serious ass kickers.

Later that day, when I saw Ben at lunch time, I asked him if he knew where the girls would be working. He smiled when he told me that my sister would be working in the Big House helping the professor and Derniere would be in the same office working on a special project. I asked him what that might be.

"Oh, just something to do with growing rice." He replied.

"In other words," I said, "she's going to be your personal assistant, you sly old dog."

Ben said, "Yes and we have to remember to call her Derniere when she's working because her grandmother didn't like her being called *Dee*. She said it wasn't dignified for an educated woman. She used to think shortening names was common and not at all proper. I remember her grandmother as one of the first women I ever saw shoe a horse and race a buggy. She was as good as the men and she had a straight razor in her pocket that she could skin a rabbit with or take a man's head off."

He went on to say, "I heard you got in a minor scuffle today with Uhuru and the girls backed you. The boss asked Arwinda why they came in two minutes late, and she mentioned that Mr. Freedom came out of the woods and held you up. Dee declared that he was lucky he got away with his manhood and that it's only because she's new here and she let him slide. I love a girl with spunk and I think that she and I are going to get along famously."

"I'm sure you will, just don't get her mad." I said, remembering the last encounter all too well.

Ben just smiled broadly, saying "You won't have to worry about that my friend. All I want to do is make her happy." When I heard that, I knew he was hooked.

～

The summer quickly passed and they say time flies when you're having fun. After the owner and Miss Daisy finally returned home to Philadelphia, I kept busy going to plenty of cookouts and hoe downs where I saw Arwinda. I also spent time with my sister, the professor, Ben and Derniere.

In September, we heard that President Lincoln had issued the Emancipation Proclamation which set free all slaves living in the States at war with the Union. By now the South had its own President, Jefferson Davis and its own constitution, which held slavery to be legal. Because of this, many of the slaves ran off to follow the Union army in the hope of getting to the North and freedom.

The only slave who left our plantation was Uhuru, and he hadn't been seen much since our confrontation so he really wasn't missed. He was waiting to ask Arwinda if she'd go with him, but she only laughed and said, "It would be like jumping out of the frying pan into the fire." She explained to us later that she felt, at least, on the island we were safe from the war and had plenty to eat. If we started following the soldiers, we'd just be begging servants asking the soldiers for handouts when they didn't have enough to eat themselves. Furthermore, everyone knew how the poor Northern soldiers treated slave women who were begging for food, and she wanted no part of that!

The summer turned into fall and around the beginning of November, we were still enjoying unseasonably mild weather. By now, The professor treated Sis as though she was already free and even a blind fool could see that all she had to do was ask and the professor, with his abundance of money, would run to the bank and buy her whatever she wanted, at any price. My sister knew this better than anyone. Because she was in a position of having work she enjoyed and paid as much as White people while working for a man who obviously loved her, she seemed satisfied to let things continue the way they were. At the same time, she was surrounded by her only family and best friend so she probably felt that things couldn't get much better.

98

Derniere was also being paid by the professor for assisting Ben in compiling a manuscript on the scientific propagation of long grain rice. This was an original idea, never done before, and the professor knew that at some point if the manuscript was copyrighted, he could sell it to other farmers across the country. He also felt that since Derniere was doing a job that he would have ordinarily paid a White person to do, she should be paid. And since he was "the boss", she was paid just as much.

The professor, wiser than most, wouldn't deal in confederate currency, which he said, was speculation at best. He insisted on venders and purchasers alike, paying him in gold coin and he paid us in the same manner.

(I often wondered if part of his motivation was that by employing us with fair wage, he gave us the means to buy our own way out of bondage when the war was over.)

One Sunday afternoon, taking advantage of the warm, sunny day, the six of us, who had become couples by then, decided to ride down to the ocean to one of the more scenic spots to have a picnic. The fact that the professor was now openly keeping company with my sister would have been somewhat scandalous anywhere else, but because he was so well known on the island, it was simply considered just another eccentricity. Of course, for a slave to have a boyfriend who was free was like hitting the jackpot since it presented a legitimate opportunity for the slave to have access to her own freedom.

When we reached our destination, a small beautiful cove on Perkins Bay, we set up our blankets on a little hill overlooking the water and unpacked a fried chicken lunch basket fit for a Nigerian king and with mouths watering, we eyed the spread like kids in a candy shoppe. There was chicken, rice, potato salad; collard greens, candied yams, sweet potato pie, watermelon, *and* Derniere brought some of her grandmother's famous monkey bread, which we covered with home-made jam.

Since Uncle Ben's hair had turned gray at an early age, everyone said he looked like a pastor; so he gave the blessing and we all dug into our Sunday feast. Barely ten minutes later when we were all beginning our desserts, a small rowboat with two of our people entered the cove. While a large man rowed, an older man, it seemed, spotted us and called out "Good morning folks. Can you give a couple of lost sailors some directions?"

The professor said, "Surely. Come ashore and we could probably help you get to where you want to go." The oarsman dug into his task and shortly the boat pulled up and the older of the two approached us. He was dressed as a sailor with wide bottom pants and a cap pulled low over his head. When he got close to us he looked at me and said, "I've seen you before, not too far back." I didn't immediately recognize him but before I could say anything the professor said, "And I've seen you but it was many years ago in Boston when you were making the rounds at Black churches collecting money for your work on the railroad, *Miss Tubman.*"

Harriet said, "Is that you, Dr. Julius? You've gained two hundred pounds since I last saw you but you were the smartest Black man at Harvard University back then and you appear to be doing very well now. We've lost our bearing in the night because of the clouds and we're trying to reach Spectacle Island."

"You're about four and a half miles due south of Spectacle Island, the professor said, but please stay and have a bite with us. That's a long pull for even the best oarsman." Harried agreed and called her companion to come up from the shore.

Harriet introduced her companion as Popeye and said that he was the best oarsman in the South, White or Black. His forearms looked like a horse's leg rippling with muscle. He wasn't the largest man I'd ever seen, but you could tell that he might well be the strongest. He called Harriet 'Olive', and while I heard she always traveled under an alias, I had never heard this one.

While they ate, we asked them how the war was going and what they thought it would mean for us. Harriet explained that while the North was losing some important battles, the South was losing more in men and supplies. She said that General Lee was a tactical genius, but he couldn't win the war by himself. Her opinion was that the North's greater resources would ultimately carry the day. She heard they were beginning to form regiments of Black soldiers; and that, in her opinion, would ultimately lead to universal manumission.

She said we should be on the lookout for soldiers from either side raiding our plantations for food. Because the war was going to be won or lost due to which side could best supply their army with guns, ammunition and food, we might well be in harm's way. Her suggestion was to tie up the ferry at night on the island so it couldn't be commandeered by the soldiers on the mainland; and when the ferry made the trip back and forth, she warned us to keep a sharp eye out for soldiers since they'd be waiting for the boat to come in.

The professor said he could handle that matter by forging a letter to the local office presumed to be sent from the main office. The letter would state that any ferry captain who lost his boat would be fined a month's pay. He figured that would keep them on their toes.

Our final question to Harriet, also known as Olive, was how soon after the war would things return to normal? She said, "The professor probably can answer that better than me. I don't personally think it'll ever go back to what we now think of as normal. If the South loses, they'll be bitter for generations. I don't think our people will have total equality for at least one hundred years, but things will get better. And because of our freedom, many of our people will prosper."

She continued," At the same time, I can see waves of folks here heading for the big cities in the North and forming an underclass of cheap labor and getting beset with all the problems that city living and poverty brings. Much like the poor White people we see now, only worse because we've been handicapped for so long. The key is education, and", she paused, her voice almost a whisper now, then continued "I believe that someday a man, who is Black, just like Dr. Julius here who's gone to Harvard University, could become the President of the United States. We can only hope!"

We gave her a small lunch to carry with her on the boat, wished her good luck and sent her on her way. Before Harriet left, she said to me, "Ty, you've certainly improved your company since the last time I saw you in that low down bar room in Savannah."

"Yes, I certainly have," I replied as I knew I was going to have some explaining to do with my sister and Arwinda. Just as she was leaving, Harriet looked at Derniere and asked "I know I could be mistaken but do you have any kin that belonged to old man Randolph?"

Dee said, "Yes. My grandmother, Constance, was sold from that farm more than twenty years ago, when the old man died. That was before I was born."

"I knew Constance more than forty years ago. Is she still walking among the living?"

"Yes she is."

"Well, I could tell you stories that would make you laugh and shudder both. She's quite a woman, but I'm sure you know that and you look just like her when she was your age. If you see her anytime soon, tell her Olive Oil was asking for her. She'll know who you're talking about. One more question before I leave. Does Constance still have that pearl handed razor she used to sport?"

"No," Dee answered, "but I have it with me right now."

Harriet waved goodbye and good luck. "Julius, you've surrounded yourself with a very impressive group. I think our people may have a chance yet, in spite of our many obstacles." As soon as she stepped into the rowboat, Popeye started pulling the oars as quickly as anyone I've ever seen and the boat nearly flew across the bay.

The women with us were impressed that both the professor and I had met the 'great engineer of the underground railroad', Harriet Tubman, and they wanted to know more about the circumstances surrounding our encounters.

Arwinda, addressing the professor, asked the first question "Dr. Julius, why was Harriet travelling by boat, when she's always associated with the railroad?" The professor responded, "I can only guess that it's part of her deception and she probably is never on a railroad."

The group then looked at me for further comments, but I could only add that I thought the professor was right because every time I had met her, she was dressed as a man and no one recognized her even though there is a large cash reward for her capture.

My sister said, "Ty, I hope you weren't drinking and spending money foolishly on fast women in that bar in Savannah."

"No Sis." I said, rather sheepishly, "I was looking for Harriet and I needed information."

Arwinda piped in, "Well if you were looking for information from fast women in low-down, honkey tonks, I hope you got as much as you needed because you won't be going back for any more." We all got a big laugh out of that; but I found it very promising since I thought of it as a good omen for our future together.

The war dragged on and time passed. It seemed that more and more of the destruction was getting closer to us, especially once General Sherman's troops marched to the sea. We realized that part of his plan was to cripple the South's economy by burning everything in his path; however, it didn't make the homeless feel any better and we began to understand what Harriet had referred to when she spoke about the bitterness lasting for generations. There were also large battles raging in Virginia and close to Washington D.C. which, until the beginning of the war, had been considered by most the beginning of the South.

While I'm sure this may sound selfish and shallow, during this same time, I was enjoying my life and spending more and more time around the people I loved most. My only concerns were that somehow the war might reach our isolated island and disrupt the good life that I'd grown accustomed to.

The mail came by ferry, which was now only running sporadically and again Harriet had been right about soldiers trying to capture it to raid our island and both sides had made numerous attempts. Without the ferry, it didn't make sense to raid the island, since there wasn't anything here except crops and how could they be carried off without a large boat? Secondly, because of the channel, you needed a large flat bottom boat which fortunately no one but us had. The Ferry Transportation Authority now stopped short of the mainland dock and put its passengers on smaller boats whenever there were more than three or four army soldiers from any side in the vicinity. In that manner, we remained safe and secure on the island as the flow of commerce and shipping to the mainland dwindled to next to nothing.

A short time before the end of the war, a letter arrived at the Big House addressed to Tyronius Coon in care of Uncle Ben and the Vanderbilt Plantation, Gullah Island, South Carolina.

When I entered the Big House that morning, everyone, except Arwinda was there, eagerly awaiting the opening of my letter with hopes that I would share the correspondence with them, at least any news relating to the outside world. I knew they were waiting for me to open the letter and I couldn't help myself from saying, "Maybe I should bring this letter back to my quarters and read it there." Of course, this put sour expressions on their faces, so I spun around and said, "Got ya!"

They waved me off and called me stupid, and my sister said, "Tyronius, you know your last name isn't Coon don't you?"

"Sure sis; but what else would you use, Vanderbilt?"

"Our father's owner's name was Johnson." She said.

"Yes," I agreed, "but that's so common that in the future they'll probably call all black men Johnson."

"Well anyway would you please open the letter and tell us what's so important that someone named Mrs. Appleby would send you a letter here in care of your so-called Uncle Ben?"

I opened the letter and read it aloud.

January 1865

Dear Ty:

I hope this letter finds you well and prosperous and having finished all your important real estate business. The money you gave me for the land you purchased came at a time when I desperately needed it and bailed me out of dire circumstances. I can't thank you enough. Also the assistance you volunteered to repair my house will be remembered fondly and I will be forever grateful.

The reason I'm writing you is to tell you that when I moved back to Savannah after my husband died, I met a gentleman through my friend, Victoria, who I have consented to marry. He is a very successful lawyer there and he believes that he will be even more so after the war is over. He claims there will be real estate deals and other claims that need legal help up the wazoo (whatever that means). Needless to say, I'm not returning to the farm and I thought that if you are going to work the 200 acres you bought, I would offer you the profit from half of the 300 acres that I still own. That is if you agree to work the entire farm.

Of course you could have the house there since I certainly won't be using it, and can't possibly take care of it or sell it, since land prices are so depressed now that the war has destroyed the South. I'm glad to be able to tell you, however, that the farm is in good shape as well as the house. When that shit-heel, General Sherman, passed he avoided our farm because he was following a nearby stream so his dirty Yankees could wash and drink our beautiful water. I'm afraid they may have to condemn that poor stream because of the filthy Yankees, but it saved our farm from ruin. Sometimes good comes out of bad. My husband said it's a good deal for me since it'll give me some spending money and keep him out of the poor house. (He's such a hoot!) I'll send you the deed to the house.

I'll wait to hear from you and I know the mail is slow as molasses these days, but everyone says the war is all but over and things should be back to normal soon.

Regards Sincerely,

I looked up at the group staring at me with mouths wide open, and I must have looked as flabbergasted as they did. My sister said, "Ty, that's what you spent our money on?" I told her it was her money I spent.

"No Ty, that was the money Mama left for both of us. I was just holding onto it until you settled down."

Derniere said, "Ty, sounds like you got yourself into a lot of monkey business and I'm not so sure you should read that letter to Arwinda." I explained this was all before I met Arwinda and then I looked at the professor and asked, "Boss, what does it all mean?"

The professor looked at me directly and declared with a straight face, "What it means is that if you can put a crew together following the end of this war, with 350 acres of farmland, you'll have a plantation, or let's call it a farm, almost as big as the plantation we're on right now. What it means is that with a little money, some good management and a bit of luck, you could be very rich. In fact, you could make six or seven of us wealthy people."

I'm not sure why, but an idea jumped into my head that between the five of us here and Arwinda, I had the makings of the best Black management team ever assembled in the Southern states of America. The professor said, "Remember this, no matter what happens, people need to eat. Cotton may have been king, but as soon as this war ends, it will be food first even if people have to wear old clothes."

I then announced, "Professor, Ben, Sis and Derniere, I'd like to talk to you all again and ask your advice about what I should do. I'm going to think this over for a couple of days and then I'd like to sit down with all of you again so you can advise me about all the things I know so little about."

My head was actually spinning. I didn't know what exactly the implications of any of the many variables the end of the war might bring. I'd heard talk about slaves, or soon to be ex-slaves, receiving *forty acres and a mule*, but most of us felt it was simply pie in the sky and wishful thinking. At the same time, if I actually wound up with 350 acres, that was enough land for eight people; and I knew, if managed well, it was more than enough land to make a great deal of money. There was also a fine large house to consider and coming from my background of servitude and bondage, that alone made me a very wealthy man considering my meager beginnings. I still had to wait to see what the end of the war would mean for our legal rights. I thought that I should talk to my sister again to see what she wanted to do about what, I felt, was her half.

～

When I drove over to my sister's place, Arwinda was there along with Dee. Arwinda said she'd heard of my good fortune and asked if I remembered that Sellamena had predicted this. I said I honestly hadn't thought about her predictions, but now that she mentioned it, I remembered every word she said. I told Sis that I had come to talk to her but the little I had to say, I could just as well say in front of her friends.

I told Sis I didn't know what the end of the war would mean, although we'd already heard Lincoln's Emancipation Proclamation and truly felt that we would soon be free. But the White people might want us gone from the South or we might have some special restrictions when it came to voting or owning property. Still we had the professor, a most valuable resource for ideas; and I wanted Sis to know that I considered her half owner of everything I'd bought including the house and the half interest in Mrs. Appleby's land, if we were fortunate enough to be able to do anything with it.

I told her, "Sis, first I want you to think about what we should do because you were always the level headed one in our family ever since our mother passed, and I respect your opinion even more than my own."

My sister looked at me like she wanted to cry and said, "Ty, you were always a good brother even though you were a little rough around the edges. When a little time passes and we see the end of this war, God willing, we'll sit down with the professor, Ben, Derniere and Arwinda and figure this out so we'll all be happy."

"Sis, that's exactly what I wanted to hear. All I want to say is 'I love you', and now I can sleep without anything troubling my mind." I said goodnight to her and Dee, and before I left, I took Arwinda aside and told her that I remembered the rest of Sellamena's predictions and hoped they would come true as well.

I slept well that night, but before the sandman caught up with me, I thought of the past five and a half years that had brought me to this point. I had dreamed in my earlier life of my owner one day setting me free. I'd never considered the politics of White men or a war being fought to separate a nation over the question of human ownership. I knew that our people were intelligent, but I never guessed that someone like the professor with a good education could be as smart as or even smarter than the Whites who owned us. For a while I never thought I'd have a pot to pee in or a window to toss it through. What a difference a day made, or at least in my case, five and a half years.

The next morning I woke up and saw Jomo's impish face at the foot of my bed. "Jomo, did you ring my bell, because I didn't hear you?"

He said he didn't have a list for me today. Nothing was going on except the war and as far as he knew, they didn't need me. He said he was here to talk to me about something serious and it didn't involve a woman.

I said, "Go ahead Jomo, I'm all ears."

Jomo had decided that what he needed was a trade and thought that driving a buggy might be a good fit for him. He thought I didn't particularly work hard, but that I got around as much as anyone and had a pretty exciting job that didn't require a great deal of hard labor. Also, to him, it seemed that because of my work, I got to carry around all the best looking ladies on the plantation, and he felt that he'd be a natural for those types of assignments. In fact, he said if I agreed to let him be my apprentice, he could start off by just taking the pretty girls wherever they needed to go.

"You have it all figured out don't you, Jomo?"

I asked him, "Are you thirteen yet?" He hesitated and replied "I will be in three months."

"Well, I'll have to clear it with the boss, but if he says it's alright, then you can start one month before your birthday. However, some of the work involves cleaning the stables and feeding and taking care of the animals. It's as important as driving the buggy; and if you can't do it or don't like it, then you cannot do the driving either. Do you understand?"

"Yes, sir, Mr. Ty," Jomo said, "and when I remind you a couple of months from now, don't get all senile on me."

"Don't worry." I said, covering my shoulder with the blanket, "Can I go back to sleep now?" But Jomo was already heading down the stairs and for once he didn't have a smart alec reply.

O nce the war ended, there wasn't a lot of rejoicing on our plantation. Most of the slaves, now free men and women had no place to go, no way to get there, and no money to live during the transition. As a matter of fact, many of the newly freed slaves had lived on this island all their lives and scarcely had enough money to afford the fare to get to the mainland, and then what? Walk to Savannah, Charleston or Atlanta, and then what? Work as a laborer? There was plenty of labor around, but most of it was in the fields and the newly freed slaves did not want to return to the work they hated and were once forced to do without compensation. By contrast, on our plantation, now called a *farm,* nobody wanted to leave because everyone had been well fed and fairly treated. Yet the problem was that no one wanted to work.

We spent a couple of weeks sitting around wondering what was going to happen once our former owner returned, until one day a letter appeared addressed to the professor from Mr. Vanderbilt.

The letter apologized for his absence and explained that due to his wife's long illness and that, coupled with the difficult nature of travel due to the war, he had been delayed much longer than he anticipated. The letter stated he was selling the farm to a large fruit company which was going to try to grow oranges and pineapples and that anyone who wanted to stay could apply for work with the new people that would show up next week. He instructed the professor to let everyone go who wasn't interested in working for the fruit company, and said they could carry as much food away with them as possible as long as supplies lasted. He said to thank everyone for their loyalty and service over the years and wished us all well in our new lives as free men. There was also a letter for Arwinda from

Miss Daisy with a check enclosed in the amount of $100.00. Miss Daisy wrote,

> *"Good luck Arwinda. When you get settled, send me your address so I can get there and buy some clothes from you. This money is to help you in your transition. You've made so many fine clothes for me since I was a child that I can never repay you. Had I inherited the farm, you would have been free long before now. I value your friendship, advice and companionship; and if you ever make it to Philadelphia, our home is always open to you. Good luck with your new life and try to hold onto that driver. He seems like a good catch."*
> *Your friend,*
> *Daisy V.*

Half of the people on the plantation left the next day for who knows where, and the other half were gone the day after. People crafted carts from large crates by adding wheels and others carried away as much as they could hold in their arms. Who could blame them? If we didn't lock and stay in the stables and the Big House, most of the belongings and commodities would have been pilfered as well. There were seven of us, including Jomo, in the Big House. I decided that evening would be a good time to discuss our future.

We had a nice dinner prepared by the three women and when it was over, the professor proclaimed, "We are all free people now so I am no longer your boss. I'd prefer that you called me Julius."

We all broke out into smiles as he continued "Ty has asked us here tonight to discuss his transition to Savannah where he owns some land. All of us, including me, will be leaving this farm soon, so any help or advice we can offer at this time is probably as good a time as any. We may not be together that much longer."

I stood up and gestured to my sister, "I hope you agree with me, but if you don't just say so and I'll go along with whatever you say." I continued, "I originally thought all I needed was advice and direction, but after thinking about this for the last two weeks, I realize that I don't need that at all. What I need and what I'd like, and I'll give everyone time to think about this, is for all of us to go to

Savannah. Together we can live in the house and work on the farm. We'll divide the money evenly, whatever the profits are, and we'll divide the cost of running the place evenly as well. We'll pay Jomo a fair wage if he decides to come and we'll also pay a fair wage to the help hired to work the farm."

"The house has five bedrooms and we can build more once we're there for a while. Between the six of us, we have enough money, talent, and expertise to run a farm and turn a profit. I've seen Julius and Ben run this place since I've been here and between Arwinda, Derniere, and Sis, we can handle the professional support, bookkeeping, staff and clothing departments. Between Jomo and me, we'll cover transportation and entertainment. All we need are laborers and we can hire them." As the others nodded agreeably, I continued "It looks to me like all of us get along well and each of us has found a partner here. If we can work together collectively, we can do very well. What do you all think?"

Dee spoke first, "When do we leave?" The rest of the group just shook their heads and smiled unanimously. My sister said, "I'm proud of you Tyronius. I couldn't have come up with a better plan."

Julius, formerly the professor, expressed that this was the most exciting thing that he'd done in years and would have been satisfied *'following Sis to a cave in the woods'*. But the idea of participating in a Black owned collective business enterprise was exactly his idea of what the new free Black community needed, and he wanted to be a part of it.

We took the two horses and carriages and loaded them with everything we thought we needed. We made the move in two days, camping out for one night. Jomo insisted on sleeping in the carriage because he had never been off the island and didn't know what type of animals lived on the mainland. I figured one of the horse and carriages belonged to me since I had stolen it fair and square from my former owner. Julius thought the other horse belonged to him since he hadn't been paid for the last two months while the war had delayed the mail. He said he brought the carriage with him when he took the job because it had heavy duty springs and he already weighed nearly 300 pounds himself.

The professor, Julius, told us to dress in our shabbiest clothes before we left. This was difficult for the women because by now all they owned was fine, custom made clothing fashioned by the hands of the highly talented seamstress, Arwinda. However, the ladies agreed once Julius explained the likelihood of encountering armed, dangerous and hungry ex-confederate soldiers who were certain to blame us for their destitution and ruin, easily making us the targets of their anger and frustration. "Further", he said, "we especially don't want to look like we're better off than they are or draw any attention at all. Besides, there are others out there, including our own people, who wouldn't hesitate to rob us."

I wasn't worried about hand to hand combat because I knew we had a secret weapon in my sister and Dee, but we didn't have any guns and we knew that we'd be at a disadvantage if we came upon any retired slave catchers or brutal ex-soldiers who blamed slaves and slavery for the fall of the South.

I surprised myself by remembering all the twists and turns that led to our new home in the deep woods outside Savannah. We arrived there safely. The only people we had passed on the road were bedraggled ex-soldiers who looked like they wanted to ask for food but had too much pride to beg from what they assumed were poor ex-slaves on the move and even more shabbily dressed than they were.

Even though the women with us had dressed down, they couldn't totally conceal their beauty and many of the White men we passed took off their hats as we drove by. Although many of these same Southern men believed in the despicable institution of slavery, in their hearts they still showed vestiges of their old Southern upbringing and gentlemanly behavior.

Once we arrived at our new home, everyone was surprised and delighted by the appearance of the house we would soon inhabit. Even I had a new appreciation since I was now looking at a grand country farm house that I owned. Because the house was set far back from the main road, no damage had befallen it other than dust and a few small rodents which Jomo quickly dispensed of. We got to cleaning the place up and decided who would stay where.

I brought Jomo with me to the stables out back to put the horses up and water them; and I showed him the quarters over the stables which he could use once we were settled in. I told him for the time being, we should probably all stay in the farm house until we knew what was what. He said that would be fine with him and that he always dreamed about having his own room. He asked if he could keep a dog with him when he moved into the stable quarters and I said sure, knowing that while we had lived in bondage few of our people could afford to feed a dog. "This", I told myself, "is going to be different."

The women, after unpacking their clothes, cleaned the kitchen with Jomo's help, and then started preparing the evening meal. After settling in, I hitched the mare up again and took Ben and Julius for a ride around our property. Ben was impressed with the land and said that with a little effort, he could have a number of crops ready by the next growing season. Julius, who was also impressed and delighted, had a speech of his own.

"Young men, my business partners, this is the future. If we can grow food here, we can help our people with jobs and feed them and everyone else at the same time. People will always have to eat, and as long as they do, we can make money. Let's buy some cows and chickens so we can have milk, butter, eggs, and poultry. In that fashion, we can be a self-sufficient farm and sell cheese and butter and eggs as well."

"If we set up a little shop for Arwinda, we can sell clothes to everyone in this area as well as Savannah. All we have to do is get her some material and find her some helpers. Derniere can handle sales of our produce and clothing, which we could keep in the same country store."

He continued, "Sis and I can be in charge of the hiring, book-keeping and day to day purchasing and payroll. Ben, of course, will handle growing and agricultural concerns while Tyronius will have to become the general foreman, or what we used to call in the bad old days, *the overseer*. At the same time, Ty would have to provide transportation around here and train Jomo as a driver so he can maintain the job when the *overseer* is too busy, which will be very soon, unless I miss my guess."

After touring the farm, we got back to our own Big House in just a little over an hour. A delicious dinner was waiting for us. Julius had copied the deed to the property and the house and posted them on the wall near the entrance door so that anyone visiting or coming by would be able to see this farm was black owned. We toasted our new life with cool water from our very own well and discussed how we were going to change the world.

While most stories end with, 'they lived happily ever after', this story does as well. However, and forgive me for rushing ahead, I'd like to list a few of the things that transpired in the next fifty years that in some way we had a hand in.

By the time we had outfitted the farm, hired some good laborers, and the first crops sprouted; the three couples, Julius and Sis, Ben and Derniere, me and Arwinda, were all married (all on the same day) and living in our own home.

We hired a preacher, even though Ben said he could do it. Our big surprise was that Sellamena mysteriously showed up and returned my lucky quarter. She said she saw our wedding in a dream and didn't want to miss the feast she knew would follow. We welcomed her and much later Derniere even named one of her daughter's after her.

For our group wedding celebration, we hired a traveling song and dance band, led by one of my old acquaintances, Beauregard Jangles. Of course, by then he went by the name of Bo Jangles.

And just to demonstrate what a small world it is, who do you think would be working for this band as equipment manager setting up their musical instruments and platform? It was none other than Uhuru himself, as big as life and twice as ugly. Seeing Sis and Derniere, refreshed his memory of what nearly happened to him the last time we met, and he instantly turned into *Mr. Nice Guy*, all smiles and congratulations. We all had a great time that day, recalling memories of our past and our hopeful future together.

Sellamena's predictions all came true. I, of course, became a real tycoon and was written up in the newspapers as the *First Black Tycoon*, at the turn of the century. My extended family laughed at that, all the way to the bank, because a lot of them became famous and made a great deal of money as well.

Professor Julius marketed a barbeque sauce that sold throughout the Eastern states, especially around college campuses. It's called Professor's Bar B.Que Sauce.

Derniere, using her grandmother's recipe, sold monkey bread to the largest Black owned supermarket chain in the South.

Arwinda made the first coon-skin hat for some senator from Tennessee by the name of David Crocket. The fashion caught on and thousands were sold. She also sold a line of African shirts for men that were big sellers in Atlanta. They were called Dashikis.

After we bought some cows, following Julius' advice, we began making extra sharp cheese on our farm and began selling it state-wide under the name '*Coon Cheese.*'

My friend, Victoria, who long ago hid me from the police in Savannah, opened a new shop called Victoria's Secrets; and I'm told she has done well with a mail order business.

Our dear Mrs. Appleby opened a bakery and became famous for selling homemade, ready to eat, Mrs. Appleby's Pies.

Lastly, my cousin has become the most famous because who hasn't heard of Uncle Ben's Rice?

A couple of years after we moved to our new home on the farm outside of Savannah, Jomo, who had grown up and become our head driver, drove to the plantation where we had lived on Gullah Island. He found Sweets, the snake man, still living there in the woods on his own. Jomo tried to persuade him to come live with us, but he was getting old and indicated that he wanted to stay and spend the rest of his life where he was comfortable with nature and where he had buried his favorite mongoose.

And one final note, Professor Julius was reading an old newspaper article one day about a White cartoonist who developed a comic series for the Sunday paper. It was called 'Popeye the Sailor Man' and reading further, it mentioned that the main character and girl-friend, Olive Oil, were loosely based on Harriet Tubman and her famous oarsman, Popeye.

It was the headline on the following page, however, which caught his attention. It read, *"Mystery of Missing Black Tycoon Finally Solved"*.

It explained that this gentleman, from Germany who spoke English, was traveling through Georgia a number of years ago with the intention of buying some cotton fields to circumvent the boycott that was anticipated prior to the Civil War. It turned out that he was way-laid, robbed and murdered by some slave catchers who had stopped a Black man earlier, who they presumed to be the *real* Black entrepreneur, and thus felt that this poor lad was a lying imposter. The article went on to say

"The full story came to light when the real Black Tycoon's signet ring was hocked in a pawn shop in Atlanta a number of years later, and was only recently put together with his disappearance. Three men are now being held in custody for the crime."

The professor showed me the article and said, "Ty, I think you might find this interesting." I couldn't have agreed more.

THE END

CPSIA information can be obtained at www.ICGtesting.com
Printed in the USA
BVOW010233121112

305196BV00005BA/3/P